Someday

Danette Fogarty

This book is dedicated to dreamers. I thank my family for understanding that I'm one of them.

Jayde Greene, a barista at a local coffee shop, is a dreamer. She was orphaned as a teenager so the regulars at the shop and her co-workers are her family. She also has a very important notebook. It's her "Someday" book that holds all of her dreams, big and small.

Parker Kinley was having a bad day and decided to stop into a local coffee shop for a much-needed break. His job as an actuary requires methodical thinking and complete professionalism. When he meets Jayde, with her hippie-like attitude and infectious smile, he's immediately intrigued and drawn in.

After meeting the enigmatic Parker, the dreams in Jayde's notebook start to come true. Is it a coincidence or love that both Jayde and Parker's dreams of Someday start now?

Chapter 1

Getting up at four in the morning might be annoying for some people, but for Jayde Greene, it was blissful. As she did every morning, she awoke to the "alarm" of Bach's Orchestral Suite No. 3. Stretching, she got up and stepped over her cat, Mr. Beethoven, who gave her a look of annoyance. Padding around quietly, she smiled. Every day was a Blessing and Jayde promised her mother long ago that she wouldn't waste one of them.

The music was now streaming through a small speaker on the bathroom counter as Jayde brushed her hair. She wore it the same way every day she worked, in a long braid that draped over her left shoulder. She was right handed and having the braid over her left shoulder kept it from falling into a cup of someone's drink or their food. It was one of those silly rituals that she just started and kept doing.

Still in her pajamas, Jayde sat down on her yoga mat. When she wasn't stretching, it was rolled up neatly and placed beside her bed. Living in a six-hundred square foot studio apartment, Jayde learned two things. One, only have what you absolutely need, mainly because there's no room for anything that isn't necessary, and two, that there was a kind of safety in feeling your whole space around you. And the space she felt was hers alone. After years of sharing a room in an orphanage or foster home, or with roommates, having space of her own was a downright extravagance.

As Jayde was doing her last couple of stretches, Mr. Beethoven sauntered over and rubbed up against the side of her leg. Smiling at him, Jayde allowed one hand to break pose to give him the desired scratching behind his ears. Something so simple, a little affection, was an honor to give.

The second alarm on Jayde's phone started playing, The Valkyrie by Richard Wagner, an instrumental song that let her know she needed to get a move on if she was going to make it to work on time.

After finishing getting dressed, and tidying up her small space, Jayde poured herself a cup of tea. She told Mr. Beethoven, "Be good," and left her apartment. She diligently locked the door and started down the stairs. Her studio was on the third floor so she was just reaching the second-floor landing when she saw her neighbor/boss's door open.

"Good morning Joe," Jayde greeted him warmly.

Joe was not a "morning person," so his answer was usually a quick nod to Jayde. Today was no exception. They walked down the next flight of stairs together and closed the door.

Jayde was lucky because her work was only about twenty feet from the door that led up to her apartment.

Joe's Cuppa Joe was a quaint little coffee shop in the downtown area of Galveston, Texas. It was in one of those renovated old buildings that used to be a factory of some sort but was now converted into retail space with apartments above it.

Joe bought the place about ten years earlier, after he retired from the Marine Corps. He was gruff and didn't look like anyone who would own a coffee shop, much less be a "people person," but he took a chance and it certainly paid off.

The shop was on the first floor, his apartment was above it on the second floor, and then he converted the third floor into two studio apartments. When he offered Jayde the job, the studio came with it, rent free, so she jumped at the chance to save money and have a job that she considered fun.

Jayde was a barista, and loved sound of the title. Before meeting Joe, she worked at a big coffee house chain. It was fun and the people were great. She was surprised when Joe asked her to come to work for him at his newly opened business. It had taken him almost six years just to complete the renovations of the shop and the apartments above and he was eager to hire someone with experience.

Although Jayde was certainly not the best barista at the coffee shop she worked at, Joe told her that he thought her personality would be a great fit for Joe's Cuppa Joe.

So here they were, the two of them, up before dawn, and getting ready to open the shop.

As if Joe wasn't enigmatic enough, he insisted on baking his own pastries for the shop. Although Jayde would admit that Joe wasn't the sparkling personality type, the man could bake better than just about anyone she'd ever met. And the concoctions he came up with were insane, but in a very delicious way.

Jayde herself was never that great in the kitchen. The microwave and ready-made soup cans were about the extent of her cooking abilities. But Joe, he just seemed to pull out these whimsically delicious recipes. Once, Jayde asked him what he did in the military, and he only replied, "Stuff I don't want you to know about." So, wherever he got his culinary skills from, Jayde could only speculate.

She was busy in the front of the shop, making sure the machines were up and going for coffee, cappuccino, macchiato, espresso, tea, and hot chocolate. As a part of her morning routine, Jayde would need to go through the back kitchen to get out the fresh milk from the main cooler. Although it was a legitimate excuse, she always tried to peek at what Joe was going to make for the day. The menu changed daily, depending on his mood and local ingredients. Only Joe knew what would be served and it was quite the selling point for the shop.

After ensuring they were set up in the front, Jayde wiped down all the display cases and started cutting up the fresh fruit that would go into cups inside of it. They only served fresh at Joe's shop and that was one thing that Jayde really took pride in.

Thirty minutes later, Joe came out of the back and brought a little plate with pastries on it. Another perk of Jayde's job was she got to be the official taste tester of any new recipe Joe came up with.

"What do we have here?" Jayde asked him.

Joe shrugged, "A citrus scone with fresh blueberries inside."

Although Jayde had tasted lemon scones and the like, she knew that Joe would have a twist on the recipe. She took a bite, and sighed. The citrus flavor filled her mouth and then there were bursts of blueberries that followed. "Yummy," She said, and smiled.

Nodding, Joe left her and went back into the kitchen.

For some people, Joe's lack of conversational skills might have been a problem. But for Jayde, she just took it as Joe being an intensely personal and quiet person. He was nice, and did talk to her, just not a lot. And, after all, that was what she was hired for, to be the friendly face of Joe's Cuppa Joe.

At 6:00am, Joe came out of the back and unlocked the front door to the shop. He gave Jayde a quick smile before returning to his baking duties in the back.

There were always a few die-hard customers who were waiting when the shop opened at six.

The hurried workaholics who ordered while they were glued to their smart phones and never gave Jayde as much as a smile.

There were the party goers. Galveston, was a tourist town so that made for a late night for some people. Most of them were funny, and still feeling the effects of the partying, so Jayde was patient. She tended to get large tips from the tourists so it was worth the extra time it might take to serve them. And some were college kids who came in to get that jolt of caffeine so they could start all over again with studying.

About eight o'clock, the "regulars" started filtering in.

There were Ray, Gretchen, and Ginny. Jayde called them her Senior Three Amigos. They were all retirees who took morning classes at the local YMCA. After the classes, they always popped into Joe's for a cup of something and a pastry.

Ray always held the door for the ladies, and Jayde thought he was so sweet for doing it.

Gretchen took the lead this morning, saying, "Good morning, Jayde," as she rushed through the door.

"Good morning to you Gretchen," Jayde replied.

She didn't just stand behind the counter because Joe's wasn't just a coffee shop, it was more like a coffee shop with a diner feel. Jayde walked over to the small table the three were sitting at and asked, "What's your pleasure today?"

Ray looked over to read the chalkboard menu that Joe wrote out daily. "I'd like one of those pepper cheese croissant things," He winked at Jayde, "and a medium coffee with cream."

Jayde nodded, wrote down his order, and looked to the ladies.

Ginny was always the last to order because she could never make up her mind. Some days she ordered three or four things just so she could try them and figure out which one she liked best. Today was different and she spoke up after Ray. "I'd like a citrus scone," She smiled shyly at Jayde, and added, "And can you ask Joe to add a small bit of whip cream on the side?"

Raising her eyebrows, Jayde made a goofy face, "I can, but you know how cranky Joe gets about people messing with his creations."

There was a shout from behind the counter, Joe yelling, "Hey I heard that!"

Jayde called back, "And am I wrong?"

After a small pause, Joe shouted, "No, but I'll give you your whipped cream, Ginny."

The little victory made Ginny so happy that Jayde couldn't help but smile. Again, the little things made the most difference.

Gretchen, who was looking past Jayde, and directly at Joe, said loudly, "Not sure there's anything on the menu that looks appealing today."

Jayde turned around, trying to hide her amusement, and saw an angry-looking Joe behind the counter. He threw up his hands, turned around, and started grumbling about, "Picky customers."

"I love getting his goat," Gretchen said quietly. "I'd like one of those chocolate and macadamia nut croissants." She looked at her counterparts and added, "And a macchiato with low fat milk."

With a serious nod, Jayde told them, "I'm on it," and went back behind the counter. She clipped the food order to the rotating rack Joe installed between the front counter and the kitchen. He took care of getting the food while Jayde did the drinks.

There were always a few display pastries, to give the customers a look, but the baked goods were kept in the back, covered and as fresh as possible. Joe believed that if you had good food, customers would stay loyal. It was another reason that Jayde respected him.

Sister Marjorie was the next regular customer who came into the shop. She was an "old school" nun and wore her hair pulled back in the most perfect bun every day. Smiling at Jayde, she sat down at a table near the front window of the shop and began reading her bible.

Jayde walked over and gave the Sister a quick hug from behind. "Good morning, Sister," Jayde smiled.

"Good morning yourself," Sister Marjorie answered. She always knew that Jayde was a Blessing and reminded her of that as much as possible. "How's it going this morning?" She asked Jayde.

With a sigh, Jayde replied, "Well, Joe has outdone himself in the scone department, I got a huge tip from a kid who was visiting from Finland, although I think it was a mistake, and Mr. Beethoven spent over an hour last night trying to cough up a hairball." Smiling, she touched Sister Marjorie's shoulder lightly and said, "It's the glamorous life I lead."

Chuckling, Sister Marjorie shook her head. "I'll say an extra prayer today for Mr. Beethoven. Those hairballs are utterly disgusting!"

Now Jayde was laughing. She always appreciated it when Sister Marjorie came into the shop. As far as Jayde was concerned, it was Sister Marjorie who made her life bearable after her mother passed away.

Jayde quickly took down the Sister's order and made her way back to the counter. She was making the cappuccino Sister Marjorie was so fond of and started thinking about her mother.

Jayde's mother was as unique a woman as they came. In Jayde's memories, her mother was this vibrant and playful woman who would take Jayde out to the park for hours or to the local aquarium. Fran, short for Francine, always wanted her daughter to know how beautiful the world and nature were. They met Sister Marjorie when Jayde was about eleven years old.

Fran was not feeling well and went to the doctor. Jayde, just a child, didn't understand why her mother had to keep going to the doctor every week. While Fran was "away" for her treatments, Sister Marjorie would sit with Jayde in the hospital waiting room. They would read or put together jigsaw puzzles or attempt those search games where you look for objects. Sister Marjorie was always so kind to Jayde and didn't even take offense when Jayde asked her about her "weird" uniform.

For all of Fran's beliefs, formal religion wasn't one of them so Sister Marjorie was the one who answered all of Jayde's questions on the subject. It was Sister Marjorie who taught Jayde about prayer and how it would help her to be strong for her mommy.

Looking over the counter, Jayde smiled at Sister Marjorie, who was still dutifully reading her bible.

It was easy to get lost in those memories, the good ones and the bad ones.

Jayde recalled how Sister Marjorie was there with her when her mom was admitted to the hospital. After two years of treatment, the cancer was winning. Fran explained to her daughter that her illness wasn't being fixed by the treatments she'd received so she was going to have to leave Jayde.

Again, Sister Marjorie brought Jayde comfort by explaining the belief of Heaven and how Jayde's mother would be there, always watching over her.

When the time came for Fran to leave, Jayde was strong and whispered to her mother, "I love you and I'll wave to you in Heaven, Mommy."

Pushing the rest of the thoughts from her mind, Jayde grabbed the honey cinnamon biscuit, with a side of butter that Sister Marjorie ordered.

As Jayde placed the plate down on the small table, Sister Marjorie looked up at her, and stated, "You were thinking about your mom."

Surprised, Jayde asked, "How did you know?"

Patting Jayde's hand, the Sister sighed. "You always have this look of longing on your face when you're thinking about her."

Even though the Sister was right, Jayde just smiled.

"It's okay to think about her, you know." Sister Marjorie told Jayde.

Jayde looked down for a moment, "I know," she smiled. "It's just that I want to remember the good things about her, not the end."

Motioning for Jayde to sit down, Sister Marjorie smiled. "It wasn't the end, my sweet girl, but a transition into something else."

Feeling surly, Jayde retorted, "I didn't want her to transition, I just wanted her to stay."

Again, Sister Marjorie patted Jayde's hand. "I know." She closed her eyes for a moment, as if contemplating something, then asked Jayde, "How about your search for your father, how's that going?"

Rolling her eyes, Jayde shook her head in defeat. "Nothing." She looked over at the table where Raymond, Ginny, and Gretchen were sitting, just to make sure they didn't need anything, and then turned back to Sister Marjorie. "Mom just didn't give me enough information to go on."

"I'll pray on it, and for you." Sister Marjorie smiled.

Getting up, Jayde looked at her surrogate mother, and replied, "I know, and thank you," before going back to the counter.

A little while later, while wiping down the counters, Jayde couldn't help but think about her life.

She was so fortunate to have what she had. A job she loved, people around her who cared, Mr. Beethoven for company, a roof over her head, clothes on her back, and food in her stomach.

And yet, for all those Blessings, Jayde felt a gaping hole in her heart. And having that hole gave her a healthy dose of guilt.

Joe came out of the kitchen, saw Jayde lost in thought, and grumbled, "Go on into the back for your break, I got the front."

Without looking up, Jayde nodded, placed the towel down on the counter, and went into the back of the shop.

There was an alcove at the very back of the space. It was barely big enough to hold a desk and chair in it. That was where Joe had his computer and did the books for the coffee shop.

Jayde sat down at the desk and opened up a side drawer. Every day she took out the notebook she kept in the drawer. On the front was simply written SOMEDAY. And inside of this notebook, was every secret dream that Jayde kept inside of her heart.

Joe gave her the drawer for her personal things so she knew no one saw her SOMEDAY journal.

She opened up the pages and flipped through until she found an empty page.

The things that went into the SOMEDAY journal were very important so Jayde tried very hard to only put in realistic things. It would make no sense to say, "Go to the moon," because that would never happen. She once wrote "Learn how to Riverdance," and although Jayde was fairly sure it wasn't even remotely attainable, she left it in.

Today, she wrote something that she'd written before in the notebook. The rules were her own, so if there were repeats then that was okay. Jayde wrote down, "Find my dad."

After a few minutes, she recalled a story she'd seen on the news a few days earlier and also put down, "Walk down the seawall every day for a week, at sunset."

The seawall was just that, a large wall that separated the city of Galveston from the Gulf of Mexico. It was always busy so Jayde tended to avoid it but now she thought the idea was worth trying.

Closing the notebook, Jayde tucked it safely back in its drawer. She supposed that most people thought it was a ridiculous thing, maybe even childish, keeping a notebook full of dreams. But those dreams gave her purpose in the moments when she felt alone.

Looking on the desk, she noticed a crossword puzzle that Joe must have started and finished it up quick. She knew it might tick him off, but Joe found most things somewhat annoying.

After her break, Jayde went out to the front of the shop once again.

As was their daily ritual, after Jayde's break, Joe left the shop. He said it was his "lunch" but he was always gone for at least a couple of hours. Again, one of those daily habits. He never mentioned where he was going or what he was doing, but it was his time so Jayde never made a big deal about it.

On Tuesdays through Saturdays, there was a part-time Barista that came into the shop at eleven in the morning. His name was Connor and he was one of the most intelligent people Jayde had ever met. His classes were Honors classes and he only went to school in the mornings because he was on track to graduate in a few months. At sixteen, that was quite the feat. Most days, Jayde could at least keep up with what he was talking about, but when he dove into the intricate workings of electronic equipment, her eyes glazed over with confusion.

Connor was sweet and considerate, and Jayde thought he was darn helpful during the late morning/early afternoon rush at the shop.

As if on cue, Connor came into the shop. He waved to Jayde, who was helping a customer, and put his ever-present back pack down in the little alcove at the back of the shop.

He was tying his apron with "Joe's Cuppa Joe" screen printed on it as he came back out to the counter area.

Thankful for the help, Jayde started calling out orders and they got to work.

Chapter 2

Later that afternoon, Connor was going over his plans for senior prom and Jayde was trying so hard not to laugh, it was so cute. He actually thought a robot he built was going to deliver a note to the girl he wanted to go with. For his sake, Jayde hoped he was successful.

More customers started to trickle in, working up to a full-blown wave within a few minutes. Jayde was surprised to see Joe come in just as the place was filling up. She sighed in relief because now she and Connor could concentrate on the front while Joe handled the food in the back.

Jayde was bussing a table near the front window when the bell on the door went off. Looking up, her usual smile of greeting plastered on her face, she simply stopped.

Everything stopped.

The man in the doorway was gorgeous, but in a completely uptight way, if that was possible. The suit he wore fitted him perfectly, his hair was in place as if he commanded it stay that way, and even his hand, as it held his briefcase, looked as if he just stepped off a page of some business magazine.

Jayde forced herself to start breathing, and managed a squeaky, "Good afternoon, just take a seat."

She started to go back behind the counter and had to practice her yoga breathing just to get herself under control. Luckily Connor was oblivious to most non-verbal communication so he didn't notice the flush in Jayde's cheeks or the fact that she wasn't actually saying anything, just staring at the man who just walked in.

As the man sat down, Jayde stared, trying to notice everything. He was graceful for a man, practically sliding into the seat of the table she'd just wiped down. He set his suitcase in the chair across from him and that told Jayde something. Either he was expecting company and, in essence, saving the seat, or he just didn't set his briefcase down on the ground. She couldn't help a sting of being insulted at the second option. They kept the shop clean!

Parker was starving and craving caffeine. The meeting he just left was a disaster, and he needed to compose himself before he went back to his office in Friendswood, Texas. The hour-long commute down to Galveston didn't bother him because business was business, but the business he was speaking of was going downhill fast, and if the owner didn't change, a once-strong company was going to fail.

Looking over at a large chalkboard, Parker scanned the food options. For the first time, he looked around the shop. It was decent size, almost cozy, and thankfully, clean. He couldn't count the times he entered a shop that served food and felt like it was just plain dirty.

Still observing, Parker didn't notice the woman come around the counter and towards him until she was only about three feet away. Because of where he was looking, he was able to see her, literally, from the floor up. His eyes noticed she was dressed casually. Her shoes were those little slip-ons that yelled "beach," her legs were long, and tanned. Her shorts were white and covered about half of her thighs. For a split second, Parker was disappointed that there wasn't more leg showing. She had a trim waist that held up a small apron. Her t-shirt was bright blue with white letters that promoted the shop, "Joe's Cuppa Joe." She wore a nametag that said Jayde. Finally, Parker's eyes made their way up to her face. If any part of her was perfect, it was her face. She wore a warm smile; her skin was devoid of makeup so Parker could see a dusting of freckles right across her nose. She had big, expressive eyes, and long hair that was braided over her shoulder. Before Parker could completely come out of his observation mode, he heard her ask, "How can I help you?" Embarrassingly enough, he couldn't answer.

Jayde wanted to giggle. This scrumptious man was checking her out. Flattering, even if it was probably going to be about a fifteen-minute mental romance. That's what Jayde called those chance encounters with the opposite sex that didn't consist of more than some warm smiles. It was a kind of side effect to her job and normally she enjoyed the innocent flirting. With this man, however, she was already bummed that all they would have is this short meeting.

He didn't answer her first offer of help, so Jayde repeated herself, "How can I help you?"

"Uh," Parker heard himself say, and then frowned. He was never tongue-tied or flustered, but this woman was making him nervous. He composed himself enough to say, "Coffee, with cream and sugar, and..."

Still smiling, Jayde waited patiently. She got the impression from him that he was a man who liked to be in control.

Parker found himself feeling unsure, not a pleasant or common feeling. "What's good?" He asked the cute server, and looked down to see her nametag read Jayde.

Giving the serious and handsome man a look of indecision, Jayde slowly smiled. "Everything here is good, I promise, it's just a matter of what you'd like." As soon as she said the words, Jayde blushed. The blatant innuendo was something she didn't often exhibit and she was embarrassed that she used it.

Now smiling, Parker replied, "I like something sweet with a little kick to it."

Jayde watched his eyes and knew he was baiting her. Feeling sassy, she replied, "I think I know what you'll like if you allow me to take a guess."

His eyes shifting quickly, he caught her gaze. A smile slowly made its way across his lips. "I'm placing my needs into your capable hands."

The atmosphere in the room changed. Jayde suddenly felt very warm. She knew her cheeks were flushed and her breathing was shallow. How did a man make you feel so self-aware with just a few words and eye contact? Jayde had no idea how he did it, only that he did it, and did it well. She couldn't answer him, nodded quickly, and turned around to get his order.

As Jayde walked over to the counter, her eyes ran into Joe's. His face said something she'd never seen before....concern. Frowning at his reaction, Jayde sighed, gave him a quick smile, and went to work getting the coffee order for their handsome customer.

Parker sat back in the chair and watched the pretty, Jayde, walk behind the counter. His eyes scanned the area and found another set of eyes focused on him. These eyes weren't pretty at all and Parker knew he was being visually warned off by the man standing in a doorway that led to the back of the shop. Parker could read people pretty well, and this man was telling him clearly, "keep away."

Breaking eye contact with the man, Parker took his phone out of his pocket and started checking voice mails.

Connor was asking Jayde a question and she didn't hear him. Her mind was focused on a certain man sitting by the front windows. Oh, he was a study in control and more polished than most people she ran into. One of the perks of her job was meeting all different kinds of people. And that led to being able to read people quickly and concisely. This man, with his high-end clothes, was the complete opposite of her. Yet, she found it fascinating that he was.

When she came out of her handsome-man-gawking fog, Jayde looked at Connor, "I'm sorry," she told him with an embarrassed smile.

Having listened to his voicemails, Parker deleted all but one, and then his eyes glided to watch the pretty waitress, named Jayde.

Jayde…. Jayde…. Parker rolled around the sound of her name in his mind. It was an unusual name and he had a sneaking suspicion that it wasn't the only thing interesting about her.

While walking back with GQ guy's order, Jayde nodded to a couple who were leaving, and then winked at Ginny. She made her way to his table and mumbled, "Okay, here's your order, is there….uh, anything else I can get for you?"

Parker's eyes lifted so they were looking into hers. There was an almost dreamy expression on her face that prompted thoughts in Parker's mind. Very personal thoughts. Thoughts that would get him into trouble if he ever voiced them out loud. Finally, he cleared his throat, and replied, "This will do for now, but stay close, I may need something else."

It wasn't the words, but the way he said them that made Jayde turn bright red. She just bet he'd need something else and, if she wasn't careful, she'd give it to him. Without saying anything, she tried to give him a quick nod before going over to where Sister Marjorie was getting up to leave.

"Thank you for coming in, Sister," Jayde squeaked out.

Trying to stifle a laugh, Sister Marjorie gave Jayde a quick hug. "I expect to hear details the next time I come in," She whispered into Jayde's ear.

Surprised that Sister Marjorie would even say something like that, Jayde turned even more red. She pulled back from the hug and gave her friend a shocked look.

"Oh please," Sister Marjorie waved off Jayde's expression, "I'm a nun, no rules saying I can't appreciate a handsome man."

Still shocked, Jayde let the word sink in. As Sister Marjorie was passing her, she spoke up, "Actually," she said, trying to say something that the Sister had told her a few years earlier about the vows that Catholic Sisters take.

"Don't split hairs," Sister Marjorie verbally cut her young friend off. "I watch Outlander, and I know what's what."

The conversation was so absurd that Jayde couldn't help herself; she started laughing.

Sister Marjorie winked at Jayde and left the shop, giving Joe a quick wave.

Parker watched the exchange between the pretty waitress and the nun and was intrigued. He wondered what the nun said to make Jayde laugh because the sound of her laughter was better than any other sound he ever heard. It was lyrical.

Once Jayde composed herself, she turned around to see the handsome man staring at her. The look on his face wasn't clear, but Jayde had the distinct feeling that it was awareness. Her cheeks were heating up yet again and she turned away from the man's gaze, just so she could start breathing regularly again.

Parker felt the moment when the pretty waitress noticed him. It was like some invisible connection linked them. His insides heated up and were acting out of control, something he wasn't used to. The response to her was making him wonder about his own sanity.

Jayde went back behind the counter and tried to get herself under control. This was ridiculous! There were a lot of handsome men that came into the shop. Almost daily, there was some hunky guy coming in and giving her a wink or smile. She stole a look over to the man sitting by the window and mentally told herself, 'That was nothing, this is the real deal.'

After helping a few more customers, Jayde knew she couldn't avoid him any longer.

She took a deep breath, and started towards his table. When she looked up, trying to gather her nerves, she noticed he wasn't there. On the table was a twenty-dollar bill and his business card. Jayde picked up the business card, and looked at it. Parker Kinley, Actuary. What was an actuary? Jayde turned the card over and found a note on the back of it.

Jayde, please call me. It was a pleasure meeting you. I'd like to see you again.

Jayde read the back of the card a few times before she tucked it into the pocket of her apron. For some reason, disappointment flooded into her mind.

The rest of the day was pretty average, the customers coming in for their late afternoon caffeine fix. At five o'clock, the shop closed. There were always the grumblings of people who wanted to stay later or get that last rush of cappuccino, but Joe was adamant. The shop closed at five o'clock, no exceptions. Connor and Jayde took care of cleaning the front while Joe straightened up the, already neat and tidy, kitchen and set out any ingredients he needed for the following day.

During her cleaning, Jayde found a tip on one of the tables. She tucked the bill into her pocket and felt the edge of the business card she'd placed in it earlier. A whole slew of thoughts skittered into her mind. Should she really call the handsome Parker Kinley? Should she play it cool? Should she really open up a can of worms that a man usually brought with him. Her thoughts were interrupted by a loud bang in the kitchen.

Connor heard the noise when Jayde did and headed back toward the kitchen with her.

They found Joe standing at the counter and a bowl of spilt flour all over the floor.

"I'm fine, just having butter fingers," Joe grumbled.

Jayde knew that you didn't mess with Joe. If he said he was okay, then he was okay. The man was a retired Marine, he was pretty capable of taking care of himself.

Both Jayde and Connor went back out into the main part of the shop and finished cleaning up.

Since the shop was kept so clean on a daily basis, it wasn't tough to keep it up. There was a sense of pride that came along with the daily chores incorporated into a small business. Again, Jayde counted herself as lucky. Although others may think working at a coffee shop was monotonous or silly, Jayde thought it was the best job in the world.

As was the case in the morning, Joe accompanied Jayde up the stairs toward their apartments. He always gave her a grudging, "Good night," and quietly opened his door, but then he would wait until he heard Jayde's door close before closing his own. It was a kind gesture that always made Jayde feel safe.

Walking into her apartment, Jayde was greeted by a very vocal Mr. Beethoven. She imagined he was telling her about his day and asking her about hers. Once she'd given him the obligatory back scratch and put out his food, she walked over to the refrigerator and looked inside.

"Is it possible to have nothing good to eat?" She asked the cat. Mr. Beethoven was busy eating his own dinner so he was basically ignoring her. Jayde thought about her "Someday" notebook and remembered that she promised to go walk the seawall every night at sunset for a week. "No time like the present to start," She commented to a, still eating, Mr. Beethoven, and grabbed her purse.

Practically bouncing down the stairs, Jayde smiled at the thought of indulging herself with a dinner out, since she was going to be on the seawall anyway.

She paused at Joe's door, debating on whether or not she should ask him to come along. Deciding that he liked his privacy, and didn't need to be bugged by her, she went the rest of the way downstairs.

In the entryway, there was a little alcove with the mailboxes for the apartments. Joe told her when she moved in that she could park her bike there to keep it inside and safe. He even installed a little bar that she could lock it to in case anyone came in.

Jayde unlocked her bike and put her purse in the small basket that was on the front. It was a beach cruiser in a pale yellow. It was simple and didn't have any gears or hand brakes. It was what Jayde liked, cute but uncomplicated. She walked it out the door and then got on.

Riding through the strand district of Galveston was like being taken back in time. The buildings were beautifully constructed and dated back to the 1800's. Jayde loved it when they decided to rehab one. Everything should always serve a purpose, at least in Jayde's mind.

She rode down a side street and waited at the light to cross Broadway. It was the major street that ran down the length of the island, virtually cutting it in half. The traffic was always a mess coming down Broadway so it took a good while and some tricky riding to get across it safely.

Once she was on the other side of the busy street, the atmosphere was all residential. It was a lovely mix of old Victorian and newly built houses. Hurricane Ike came through in 2008 and did some significant damage to the island. Jayde shook her head as she passed houses that still weren't rebuilt after that horrible storm.

Making her way toward the seawall, Jayde tried to just take in the coastal breeze that was picking up, and trying not to think about anything in particular. "Thinking is overrated," her mother used to tell her. Although Jayde didn't necessarily agree with that, she tried to find a happy medium between thinking enough to keep herself on the right path and trying not to make herself crazy with distractions.

The seawall was, as usual, teeming with tourists. It was the height of summer break and Jayde rode past Pleasure Pier, smiling at the sounds of kids yelling as they rode the rides.

Standing at a light, waiting to cross the major boulevard that was also called Seawall, Jayde had a mental picture of Parker Kinley pop into her head. She wondered if maybe he liked to walk along the beach. Mentally telling herself to, "stop it," Jayde crossed when the light told her to.

There were plenty of distractions after that. People on bicycles, or pedaling the group bikes you could rent. The sidewalk was up above the beach, on top of the "wall" that protected the city from the Gulf of Mexico. People walked along, trying to find a place to eat or schlepping back to their hotels after a day at the beach. Parents trying to corral kids who wanted to "stay a little longer." It was very busy but that still didn't stop her from wondering if Parker Kinley would like to join her.

Periodically, there were bike racks set along the seawall so Jayde found one to lock her bike to and walked down the nearest set of steps that led down to the beach. Her Someday list was to walk the seawall for a week straight at sunset, but she longed to feel the sand under her toes. She might even dare to dip her feet in the water at some point.

After walking for a few minutes, she found an empty space in the beach and plopped down.

Allowing the breezes off the coast to caress her skin, Jayde sat there for a long time. The sunset was technically off to her right, but she still watched as its rays drifted downward, casting shadows along the wall. She closed her eyes and just listened….to the water as it crashed onto the shore, to the people who were trying to get packed up from a day at the beach, to the traffic as it whizzed by on the road above.

All the sounds made her feel a little lost because she wasn't technically a part of it.

Her mother would tell her that she was a part of everything, of course, but she really wasn't. Jayde's life was rather sheltered these days and she was pretty sure it was because of her fear after her mother passed away.

Trying not to get dragged into the memories of grief, Jayde opened her eyes. She saw a man running down the beach, his trim body seemingly drifting along the edge of the water, and she thought of another handsome man named Parker Kinley.

Chapter 3

When Parker returned to his office, in Friendswood, he tossed his suitcase onto a nearby chair and sat behind his desk. There was a stack of messages on his desk, so he skimmed through them. Disappointment snuck up on him when there wasn't one from a young woman named Jayde. He'd spent the drive up from Galveston thinking about her in her little white shorts and freckled nose.

It was a little disturbing to Parker that this woman was able to occupy his thoughts so much that he barely remembered the drive up from the island. Not a usual thing for someone like him. He maintained a lot of control in his life and for something to take up this much of his brain power, it had to be significant.

His assistant, Owen, came into the office. Parker hired him through a recommendation of a friend, and was glad he did. The kid was as detail-oriented as Parker and had a sharp mind. He was still in college but was undecided what to pursue. His job with Parker was supposed to help him get focused.

"Hello boss," Owen addressed him.

Rolling his eyes, Parker gave the kid a small smile. He understood that he was seen as an uptight person by most people so having Owen around, with his good-natured ribbing, and youthful outlook, softened up the perception a little. Even his parents told him to, "lighten up a little," every now and then.

Normally, Parker would blow off the opinions of other people, but after meeting Jayde, the pretty waitress, he wondered if the advice wasn't warranted. Without thinking, he asked Owen, "Am I too serious?"

The question threw Owen off his proverbial seat, "Uh, yeah," he answered, and then thought he'd answered wrong when his boss frowned deeply. "You're in a serious profession, it warrants a serious attitude."

Parker knew the kid was backtracking with his answer, but he appreciated the honesty. "I met a girl," He paused, "I mean a woman," he paused again, "in Galveston and she's not serious like me," he paused again, "at least, I don't think so. She seemed...."

Owen was standing there, gawking at his boss. The great and powerful Parker Kinley was distracted....by a woman....

It took Parker about half a minute to realize that what he'd said really surprised Owen. He asked himself, 'Is it that surprising that I would meet a woman?'

Now, seeing his boss' nervousness, Owen cleared his throat. It was time to lay it out there. "Listen boss, I think you're a great actuary. People who call are looking for the best, and I think it's you. But you gotta admit, wild and crazy isn't your regular modus operandi."

"I suppose not," Parker replied, and was given a shocked look by his assistant.

Sitting down, Owen tried not to laugh. "Okay, so you met this woman, and she's like...." He paused so his boss could fill in some blanks.

A smile stole across Parker's lips as soon as the mental picture of Jayde came into his mind. "She's a waitress at a coffee shop in Galveston," He explained.

"And?" Owen asked, sure that by now, Parker would've gotten everything but her social security number.

Moving his eyes so he was looking at Owen, Parker answered, "That's it."

Shocked, and knowing his face showed it, Owen stood back up. "Uh, okay," He mumbled trying to exit the office. "I'll let you get back to work."

Parker couldn't believe his assistant was this quiet. Owen never passed up an opportunity to give his opinion, solicited or not. "Hey, wait," He called out.

Owen slowly backed into the office, "Yes," he turned slowly so he was facing his boss again.

"I left my card, and a note for her to call me." Parker advised him, hoping that made him look less uptight. If Owen's expression meant anything, it didn't. "I should have done something else?" He asked.

Shaking his head, Owen sighed. "Uh, yeah," He began, "you should have gotten her phone number, planned a date, something." He gave Parker a skeptical look, "I'm not sure just leaving your card was good enough. Women are sophisticated and want to see some interest."

If Parker wasn't the man he was, he'd explain to his young protégé that what passed between him and Jayde was way more than a few looks. There was awareness there that he'd never felt before. If Jayde didn't feel it too, Parker would be shocked. "So, what you're saying is…."

"I'd call that coffee shop, ask for this Jayde, and ask her out on a date." Owen offered.

Parker nodded, and took the advice under consideration. In matters of business risk, he was definitely the best man for the job. But, in matters dealing with women, he would have to concede that Owen was far more in tune with what the opposite sex wanted.

Looking down at the pile of messages, Parker realized that he had to focus on work right now and think about his move with Jayde later. He picked up the phone and dialed the number on the first message.

Jayde found a food truck parked down the seawall and grabbed a taco and a small water. She was hungry but didn't want to eat too much and not feel good riding her bike back home.

The food filled her belly and was delicious. She began walking back towards where she locked up her bike, her water bottle in one hand. She was a few yards from her bike when a horn honked. Jayde turned to see her friend, Felicia, pull up.

"Hey there," Jayde smiled.

Felicia smiled, "Hey there yourself," she asked, "do you need a ride?"

Jayde shook her head, "No, I've got my bike. Are you going to get out and walk?"

Laughing, Felicia shook her head no. "I'm on my way to a dinner date. Dating app set up."

Her friend didn't look as thrilled as she should, in Jayde's opinion. "Why are you going?"

Felicia answered, "We're not all just going to have some handsome guy walk in and say, "Hey," are we?"

Immediately Jayde thought of Parker Kinley. "No, I guess not," She told her friend and then waved as Felicia pulled away.

Pulling out the business card that Parker left on the table of the shop, she sighed. It was scary, calling someone out of the blue, even if they did give you their number.

Parker was pulling into his driveway when his cell phone rang. He didn't recognize the caller I.D. so used his business voice, "Parker Kinley."

'He sounded so proper,' Jayde thought to herself. "Parker, this is Jayde," Her tongue almost tripped over her own name. "We met at the coffee shop earlier today."

As soon as she spoke, Parker knew who she was. His pulse started to speed up. "Yes, I remember," His voice dropped and then he closed his eyes, embarrassed. He didn't need to sound like some pervert on the phone.

"Well," Jayde laughed nervously, "you told me to call you."

There was a silence. It only lasted a few seconds, but Parker was truly at a loss for words. "Well, I did, yes," He was babbling, "Um, I wanted to," he was trying to build up his nerve. "That is, I wanted to ask you out to dinner." There, it was out!

Smiling, Jayde knew he was nervous. She was too and that made it much easier to answer. "Yes, I'd love to."

"Great," Parker rushed, "How about tomorrow night?"

Nodding, and then realizing Parker couldn't see her nodding, Jayde spoke up, "Yes, that would be nice."

Mentally listing the restaurants he was familiar with; Parker then asked if Jayde like to go out to a popular steak place he liked in

Galveston. His voice wasn't as steady as it should have been but Jayde made him feel very unsteady.

They agreed on a time and that Parker would pick her up at the shop. She didn't offer any information about living above it or anything else that was personal. After all, a girl had to be careful.

Once she'd hung up with Parker, Jayde noticed her steps were lighter. It was kind of exciting to see someone new. To daydream about the awareness, she already found with him. Her mother would probably think she was crazy. Parker Kinley was the exact opposite, at least from appearances, from what her mother always described as, the best kind of partner.

Memories of the past came up again. Jayde allowed them to come again. These were happy memories of her mother.

"Momma," Jayde asked when she was eight years old. They were sitting at the dinner table and talking about their day. Jayde loved to tell her mom about school and her classes. Fran always listened intently when her daughter spoke, and Jayde remembered the good feeling of having that constant support. "In class today, we were asked to do a family tree."

Jayde remembered how quiet her mother became. After, what Jayde could conclude now, was time to think about the answer, Fran replied, "And you'd like to know about your father?"

It was something they didn't talk about too much. Jayde learned at an early age that her mother didn't know much about her father. She'd been a curious child and normally Fran supported the trait, unless it had to do with Jayde's father. Fran was uncharacteristically quiet about the subject.

With a small nod, Jayde waited patiently. She would be disappointed once again when Fran stayed quiet on the subject.

Finally, Fran said something. "He was a tall man. He had broad shoulders that made him look very strong. And," Fran paused and sighed. "He made me feel so special."

Watching the dreamy look her mother wore on her face, Jayde felt that her mother really loved her father. It took a bit of the sting out of the feeling of not having a dad around.

Jayde snapped out of her memories. Her life was what it was and it made Jayde happier than a lot of people she knew. It was something. And now, with the anticipation of her date with Parker, it was pretty exciting.

Parker was walking through his house, which as a neat and tidy as he was. Everything had its place. His mother called it stark, but he considered it minimalistic with a touch of class. At least, that's what the decorator he hired told him.

As he was walking through the large living room, he wondered what the free-spirited Jayde would think of it. All of the furniture was a light beige with clean lines. The decorative pillows were done up in varying shades of browns. The stone fireplace that was the centerpiece of the room, was sleek and smooth marble. For the first time, Parker agreed with his mom, it did look stark.

The next morning, Jayde came down the stairs and met with a quiet Joe. Normally, she would just think it was his personality, but today something seemed a little off. "Are you okay, Joe?" She asked him as they were walking downstairs.

Joe was thinking. A pretty self-contemplative person on a regular basis, he wasn't prone to long conversations. And last night, he'd done more thinking than he was comfortable with. Even Jayde's bright and cheery attitude couldn't shake the feelings he was experiencing. With a grumbled, "I'm fine," he hoped she would just let it go.

Jayde watched Joe and knew he was mentally grinding on something. It wouldn't do her any good to bug him about it, he'd just turn more inward and not say anything at all. Trying to respect his attitude, she just smiled and continued downstairs.

They opened the shop and went about their morning. Joe brought out some muffins and Jayde wanted to just sigh when she tasted them. They were chocolate, with white chocolate covered pretzels inside. There were cranberry and walnut scones, and surprisingly, a pineapple and ham biscuit.

Joe mumbled, "A little Hawaiian today."

Looking at Joe, Jayde gave him a warm smile. "I think we should call it Lei Biscuit."

Chuckling, Joe nodded. Having Jayde, who was so different from him, was a breath of fresh air. She was a light that brightened up any room she walked into.

When he approached Sister Marjorie at the VA hospital, years earlier, and told her about his coffee shop, she recommended Jayde. He didn't know at the time how much of a difference Jayde would make in his business and in his life. She was the daughter he never thought he could have. He wasn't unaware at the looks she and that overly-handsome customer shared yesterday. Although the years passed, it seemed like just yesterday when he was gazing at the young women in the same adoring way. It was just this side of uncomfortable to see that man look at Jayde that way. Joe considered himself her protector and that man had "heart break" written all over him.

The rest of the morning went according to schedule and Jayde was having a good time laughing at the story Ginny was telling her about a funny mishap during the senior water aerobics class when she heard the door chime. Looking up, Jayde's smile got stuck on her face. It was Parker Kinley.

Parker had another meeting scheduled this morning with the same company he met with yesterday. They took his suggestions into consideration and were going to move frantically to try and save their business. It made Parker feel good about his abilities when he was able to help someone. Since he was here, it seemed a shame not to pop into the local coffee shop for a quick cup.

He visually scanned the shop for Jayde and smiled when he saw her. Her hand was on the shoulder of a woman she was talking to. She was laughing and when she saw him, stopped. Once again, the feelings he felt yesterday bubbled up and he was struck with the overwhelming reaction.

Jayde watched as Parker gave her a smile and found the same seat he was at yesterday. Smiling as she walked over to him, Jayde thought he was probably a creature of habit in most things. She got to the table and asked, "Two days in a row, is this becoming a habit, Mr. Kinley?"

As he looked up at her, Parker certainly hoped so. "I was in the area for business and wanted to try something good. What did your boss make today that's irresistible?"

Innuendo dripped off of their words and it made Jayde's insides scream in delight. "Well, I happen to be a huge fan of the pun so we've got a Lei Biscuit that will make you wish you were in Hawaii." She pointed to the menu list.

Parker laughed, "Okay, let me have the biscuit that will make me want to walk in the white sand of Waikiki and drink Mai Tais."

"You sound like a man who's actually done those things," Jayde told him, curiosity brimming.

She was a very intriguing woman. Parker smiled, "Yes, as a matter of fact, I have been there."

Glancing around the room, Jayde made sure that no one else needed help, then slid into the chair across from him and asked, "Tell me about it?"

The question was as much of a surprise to Parker as Jayde was. "Uh," He started, "well, you can smell the salt in the air if you're within a mile of the Pacific." He watched her focus and wanted to give her a good story. "The forests are so green and lush and even if it rains, you don't mind it, you only watch as the rain etches waterfalls out of the green mountains."

Jayde sat there, her chin in her hand, and wondered why the man was in a serious job. She googled actuary the night before and thought it fit him, at least his appearance, of being someone in control. Now, he seemed like a mystic storyteller, weaving such a vivid picture that Jayde swore she could feel the breezes or see the waterfalls. "Wow," She whispered, longing in her tone.

Parker found himself in a crazy position. He was torn between wanting to just look at her and keep telling her about his adventure in Hawaii. It was his parents' gift to him for college graduation. At the time, he thought it would be a waste of time to go and sit on an island for a week and "relax." Parker didn't ever really relax, it just wasn't his thing. But he suspected that Jayde would've enjoyed the experience. "Well, it was pretty spectacular."

They sat there, looking at one another for a minute.

Hearing Joe call her name, Jayde broke the visual connection first. "I, uh, guess I'll go get your biscuit."

When Parker left about fifteen minutes later, she felt even more excited about their dinner date this evening.

Chapter 4

As soon as five o'clock came, Jayde was locking the door. Normally she didn't mind if people stayed a little longer, but tonight she wanted to get home in time to get ready for her date with Parker Kinley. Just saying his name in her head made her feel like giggling.

Although Connor didn't notice her change in mood, Jayde was pretty sure that Joe did and he did not approve. He watched her like a hawk and gave Parker a couple of sharp looks. And even if Jayde did appreciate Joe's protective instincts, she didn't necessarily want him to run off every guy who showed an interest in her.

She quickly wiped down tables that customers vacated just before closing and made sure the cash register was reconciled while Connor took care of cleaning the floor.

Joe came out of the kitchen about five-thirty and told them both to "Get a move on," so the three of them left right after that.

As Jayde waved goodbye to Connor, she turned around to find Joe looking at her thoughtfully. The man clearly had something on his mind.

"Joe," Jayde began speaking as they walked toward the doorway to their apartments, "I get the distinct impression that you have something to say to me."

Opening the door for Jayde, Joe waited for her to precede him, then he grumbled, "Not my place to say anything about who you spend time with."

She couldn't help herself, Jayde smiled. "And yet, you give this man a not-so-subtle look of "hands off" when you see him."

They were making their way up the stairs now and Joe stopped to look up at Jayde. "I'm protective of you. Sister Marjorie told me how it was for you and I just want you to be happy."

Astonished, Jayde just stared at him for a full minute. Never, in the years she'd known Joe, had he ever said anything about what prompted him to hire her or about her happiness. It was like seeing an abominable snowman, it was so unlike him. "Well," She spoke when she could get her voice, "I can't tell you how much I appreciate your interest in my happiness." She reached out and patted his arm, "And I'll make you a deal, if this guy does anything that is even remotely bad, I'll let you know so you can do something that I can't even dream up."

Joe, looking so serious at first, surprised himself and smiled. "Deal," He announced, then motioned for her to continue up the stairs.

Jayde opened the door to her apartment, found Mr. Beethoven in his usual place, and smiled as she went into the bathroom to get ready for her dinner date.

Parker was putting on his fifth tie and was still frustrated. He forgot to pick up his dry cleaning so the shirt he planned to wear wasn't in his closet. There was a new client who stayed at the office longer than scheduled so he got home late. There was yet another message from his mother demanding that he call her and confirm that he was still among the living. And now, every tie he tried on wasn't right.

Tossing the piece of fabric into the growing pile, Parker walked over to the mirror. "You're nervous Kinley," He admitted out loud. "This isn't a business meeting, this is a date with a beautiful woman."

After hearing himself speak, Parker realized he was overreacting. Deciding to forego the tie, he unbuttoned the top button of his shirt, and grabbed his jacket.

The drive down to the island was anything but pleasant. The traffic going southbound was a mess this time of day and Parker couldn't believe he forgot to calculate that.

Jayde was giving herself a final look when her phone went off, saying she had a text message. It was from Parker…

Traffic is horrible, I may be a little late.

Smiling at his consideration, Jayde typed back.

No problem.

She decided to turn on some music to help pass the time.

By the time Parker pulled up in front of the shop, he was frazzled. If the traffic wasn't bad enough, he'd dumped water on his jacket. He threw it in the backseat and got out of the car in a huff.

When he turned around, he stopped. There, on the sidewalk, stood Jayde. Only this Jayde did not reflect the carefree young woman who worked at Joe's. This woman was sophisticated and made his level of nervousness take a step up. "Jayde," He barely croaked out as he came around the car. "You look lovely."

There was something about the calculated way Parker spoke his words that made a tingle work its way up Jayde's spine. She smiled warmly, and answered, "Well, Mr. Kinley, I appreciate the fact that you went without the tie."

Absently moving his hand up to his collar, Parker smiled. All the things that seemed to go wrong earlier disappeared. "And you let your hair down."

Jayde smiled again and stood there, waiting.

As if he'd been out of practice in being a gentleman, Parker took a few moments before realizing he needed to guide her to the car and open the door. "Uh.....let's get going, shall we?"

He guided her the few steps to the car and opened the door. After she was inside, he jogged around the car and got into the driver's seat.

They went to a popular steak house just minutes away from the shop. Although Jayde had never been there, she'd heard a lot of great things from customers who came in.

Standing next to Parker as they waited to be seated, Jayde studied him discreetly.

Parker waited impatiently, trying to understand how everything was going so far off the rails. "I'm sorry," He whispered to Jayde. "I pushed back our reservation when I realized I would be late, but I guess they're pretty busy."

Putting her hand on his arm lightly, Jayde replied, "It's no problem, Parker, I love to people-watch and this gives us a few minutes to talk before we're forced to stare at one another across the table."

She was half way through her words when Parker caught on to her joking. He smiled. "I love the way you say my name," He blurted out before he could think.

Jayde put her hand over mouth quickly to tamp down on the urge to giggle. It was obvious that he didn't mean to say the words out loud.

"Well, I'll be sure to say your name a lot then," She answered, trying to put him at ease.

Thankfully they were called to be seated.

When the server left with their drink orders, Jayde gave Parker a thoughtful smile. "I thought I would be nervous." She told him.

Surprised by the admission, Parker laid down his menu. "Really?" He asked.

"It's just," Jayde paused, "you're so proper and businesslike, and I'm so not." She was blushing.

Her honesty made Parker smile. "Why do you think I'm a certain way and you're not?" He waited for her eyes to meet his. "Is it because I wear a suit or because I'm a snob about putting my briefcase on the floor?"

Now Jayde did giggle. "You do dress rather snappy."

"Snappy?" Parker snorted. "Who uses that word?"

Her eyebrows raised, Jayde answered, "Apparently I do. It just seems to fit you."

Parker nodded reluctantly.

Resting her chin on her hands, Jayde leaned closer, and said, "And I did notice the snob thing about your briefcase and I can tell you, the floor of Joe's Cuppa Joe is immaculate."

Feigning fear, Parker put up his hands. "Duly noted." He told her, then laughed.

All the tension about being late, his wardrobe malfunctions, and the delay in dinner was washed away. Parker found himself enjoying Jayde's company for the sheer joy of being around her personality.

"So," Parker said, "Tell me about what makes Jayde.....well, Jayde."

The statement made Jayde laugh outright. "Well, no pressure there," Jayde retorted. "Where do I begin?"

Allowing Jayde the time to begin, Parker took a drink of his water, and waited.

"Are we going in chronological order, in order of life experiences, or just most recent stuff?" Jayde asked him, trying to delay talking about herself.

Putting his hands out, palm up, Parker silently told her to begin wherever she liked.

With a sigh, Jayde started, "Well, I'm from Texas, born up north but my mother and I moved down here when I was nine. My dad was never in the picture so it was just Mom and I."

Even though he wanted to give her platitudes of condolences, Parker figured she wouldn't appreciate it. She was giving him the facts so he stayed quiet and listened.

"When I was eleven my mom got sick." She took a breath, "It was cancer." Smiling at Parker to let him know she was okay, Jayde continued. "She was in and out of the hospital and that's when I met Sister Marjorie."

Parker recalled the nun that said something to make Jayde laugh.

Looking down at her hands, Jayde smiled and said, "Well, mom lost her battle when I was thirteen." She put up her hand when Parker started to say he was sorry. "It was hell, I won't lie."

It was difficult to watch the grief as it played across Jayde's features. Parker felt his chest tighten up and couldn't understand why his reaction was so intense.

"I was in and out of foster homes and a group home, but I finished high school and one year of college." Jayde took a sip of her water before going on. "I couldn't quite figure out what I wanted to do and college would be a waste of time and money until I did figure it out."

Her words made Parker stop and think. For him, college was a foregone conclusion. His parents just expected him to go so he went. They probably weren't thrilled with his choice of professions, but they still supported his goals.

Jayde smiled, "And then I was working for a chain coffee house and in walks Joe." She remembered it vividly. "The warm and charming soul that he is, I just couldn't resist his offer of a job."

Parker could hear the sarcasm in her voice regarding Joe, but he also heard genuine caring in her words.

"I've worked at Joe's since and I love it." Jayde told him and smiled.

Jayde spoke about Joe, Connor, her Senior Three Amigos, and Sister Marjorie. Jayde was impressed with Parker's attention. He asked her questions that meant he was really listening. Finally, it was Jayde's turn to ask about him.

"And you...." She smiled at Parker, "What makes you so dapper?"

Giving Jayde a fake grimace, Parker tried to think of something that he could say. "I'm afraid of sounding like a boring guy," His tone was dry.

Jayde smiled, "I had to look up actuary, is that something you always wanted to do?"

Now Parker was in his element. "No," He replied, "I actually went to college to be a CPA and ended up spending a summer interning for an Actuary." He winked at Jayde. "I had to look up actuary too."

It was difficult not to smile when Parker was being so charming, so Jayde didn't even try to look serious.

"Anyway, I liked it. It's a bit like gambling but with numbers and numbers don't lie so it's like hedging your bets on a sure thing." He stopped, and realized how awful that sounded. "I'm not a gambler by nature so I'm not sure why I used that analogy. I guess I'm trying to impress you even though no woman I've ever met showed even the slightest interest in my work."

He seemed to run out of steam and stopped talking. Jayde thought it was a shame since listening to him speak was almost as interesting as what he actually had to say.

"Well," Jayde said with a smile, "their loss is definitely my gain Mr. Kinley."

Parker found his body responded to certain tones in her voice. The inflection of her words or when she said his name just drove him nuts, in a wonderful way.

Leaning forward, Jayde asked him, "Do you think there is something wrong with me working as a barista?"

Her question threw Parker a bit. Was this a trick question? "Uh, no," He replied. "I think you should do what you love. Lord knows not many people understand my profession and I just think it's their loss." He took a small sip of his wine, preferring to remain sober since he was driving. "I guess there are quite a few people who may view our chosen professions as something "less" but I like it that we don't back down. A bird of a feather type thing."

The analogy made Jayde laugh. "I think you may be right, Mr. Kinley."

Parker cocked his head to the side and gave her a thoughtful look, before asking, "What's with the Mr. Kinley thing?"

Jayde bit her lip while she considered her answer. "Easy," She explained, "I think of you as someone who exudes business and power."

"Are you trying to stroke my ego, Ms......?" It occurred to Parker that he didn't know her last name. "Um, I'm embarrassed here because I only know that Jayde is your first name.

Here it comes, Jayde thought, the inevitable teasing that people gave when they heard her name. "Jayde Greene," She told him in a quiet voice.

A slow smile came across Parker's face. "Perfect," He stated.

Jayde's eyes flew to his, shock was evident in them. "No joking or good-natured ribbing?" She asked him.

Shaking his head, no, Parker answered, "Why would I, it's the perfect name and your mom was brilliant for giving it to you."

"Thank you, Parker," Jayde said quietly, making sure she used his first name.

With a warm smile, Parker replied, "You're most welcome, Miss Greene."

The rest of dinner was spent talking about crazy things they both encountered in their jobs. They discussed how people viewed them normally and how much they both tried to be thankful for the Blessings they were given.

Jayde was relieved when Parker didn't feel that her relationship with Sister Marjorie meant she was "preachy" or "self-righteous." Those were descriptions she'd heard before from men she'd dated and it didn't sit well.

After dinner, they were walking out to Parker's car when Jayde asked him, "Would you like to walk down the Seawall with me tonight?" She smiled, "I said I'd do it every day for a week and really want to keep my promise."

It was easy to nod yes when Parker didn't want their time together to end. First dates were stressful enough, but when you met someone that you really liked, it was tough to say goodnight. "Sure," He told her and opened up the passenger door to help her into the car.

The drive from the Strand side of the island to the Seawall only took about fifteen minutes but the time was filled with talk about the island, it's history and architecture, with Parker asking most of the questions.

By the time they found a space to park on the Seawall, the sun was beginning its quick decent toward the horizon. The wind was picking up as the daylight dimmed but the heat of the summer was still thick in the air.

Parker pulled into the first parking spot he found, shut off the car, and walked around to help Jayde get out.

They began walking down the wide sidewalk that topped the Seawall itself.

Neither of them spoke for a while, choosing to just enjoy the scenery and watch the waves as they caressed the beach.

"How am I doing?" Jayde asked him when they were about a quarter mile away from the car.

He gave her a quizzical look and asked her, "What do you mean?"

With a sigh, Jayde explained, "Well, first of all, first dates are about getting to know the other person to see if you want to actually see them on subsequent dates." She smiled shyly and went on to say, "So, I'm just clarifying that I don't have any horrible eating habits or have food stuck in my teeth, or anything else that might make you question whether we might have a second date."

Her speech was so unexpected that Parker didn't have time to digest it before he started to laugh. When he saw that his laughter embarrassed her, he quickly stopped. "I'm so sorry, it wasn't that what you said was wrong in any way, it was just that it was so honest and I think you're doing great."

Although his laughter definitely started to make her nervous, his words did a lot to soothe her concerns. "Good, because I'd like to see you again, Parker Kinley."

Chapter 5

The next morning, when Jayde's alarm went off, she stayed in bed for just a few minutes, thinking about the night before.

Parker was a gentleman, he walked her to the door leading up to the apartments, wished her goodnight, waited for her to go inside, and then left.

Recalling the moment, Jayde wished he would've kissed her.

Not that she went around kissing men. She was probably considered a prude on some level, and was very selective about the men she dated, and especially about the men she chose to be intimate with. There weren't very many, but Jayde liked to think she had adequate experience in determining a man's interest. Now she wondered if Parker was thinking the same thing.

Owen unlocked the door to the office and frowned. He made it a point to get there at least twenty minutes before his boss so he could make a fresh pot of coffee. Parker seemed to appreciate his efforts so it was kind of a daily ritual. This morning, when he pulled into the parking lot, he noticed that Parker's car was already parked in its regular spot. There was a smell of coffee in the air so Owen knew Parker took care of the coffee chore already.

After putting his backpack down behind his desk, Owen went into the doorway of his boss' office. Parker's head was down and he was engrossed in a report he was reading. Owen cleared his throat, and said, "Good morning. I guess you wanted to be an early bird this morning."

Parker was so into the paper he was reading that he didn't hear Owen come in. Very strange. Although, since last night, a lot of things were very strange.

His mind immediately drifted to Jayde, her face filling his mind. After their walk, he'd taken her home, only to find out that she lived above the shop. When it was time to say goodnight, he tried to do the honorable thing and make sure she went inside before he left. What he didn't count on was having an empty hole in his chest when she went inside. The evening was great and Jayde was so much more than what he expected. She was funny, charming, and a complete surprise with her honesty.

Coming out of his "post-date trance," Parker looked at his assistant. "I'm just eager to get things wrapped up today." He put the paper he was reading back into the client's file and tapped the file on the desk, before telling Owen, "Hey, can you hold my calls for about half an hour or so? My mom has been harassing me to call her and I might as well get that over with this morning."

With a quick nod, Owen left the office and closed the door behind him.

Parker dialed his parents' home and waited. He knew his mother would be home. It was a weekday and she worked from home. She was an editor for an online women's magazine and she was a cutthroat in her industry. She believed in putting one hundred percent into everything she did. Parker believed that she was the one who gave both him and his brother the drive they had in their respective careers.

Silvia Kinley was at her desk, editing an article, when her phone rang. She normally didn't take calls on her personal phone during business hours, but it was her son. She picked up the phone and pushed the accept button before greeting him with, "Well, it's good to know you haven't fallen off the face of the earth. Dad and I were wondering if we should organize a search party."

Parker smiled at her tone, and retorted, "Says the woman who left us for an African Safari for two months in the hopes of getting an interview with a dictator who had a fondness for eliminating crazy reporters."

Brushing her hand in the air, Silvia smiled, "I'd say you haven't lost your dramatic tendencies."

"Hi mom," Parker said dryly. "How have you been? Good, that's great. I've been good too, just working a lot. Okay, it was great talking to you." He rambled quickly in the hopes that his mother would be so busy with work that his feeble attempts at conversation would placate her for the time being.

Considering what her son was saying, a slow smile spread across Silvia's lips. "Oh, you've met someone," She quietly stated to her son.

Sometimes, in the recesses of Parker's mind, he wondered if his mother was psychic. The woman seemed to know things about her children that defied a simple explanation. "Maybe," He replied. "I may have gone out with a young lady just last evening."

Still smiling, Silvia asked, "And does she think my son is as handsome and successful as I do?"

"I'm not sure anyone could hold a candle to you, Mom," Parker said to her. "She's a very….," His voice faded off as the thoughts of Jayde filled his mind.

Now that her son had her undivided attention, Silvia turned away from her computer. Parker was not a man who had a loss for words, on any subject, so the fact that he couldn't finish a sentence about a woman he'd met spoke volumes. "She must be something," Silvia spoke slowly.

Considering his mother's words, Parker smiled. "She is," He answered, then felt uncomfortable about spilling his guts to his mom. "Well, have I met all the "mom requirements" for a phone call?"

Silvia smiled, "Yes, I suppose," she replied, then added, "But please call me within the next month." Smiling into the phone, she told Parker, "It's just to pacify me, and I appreciate your effort."

Parker chuckled. His mother tried to make every call, even personal ones, sound like business. "Got it, Mom. Can you please tell Dad that I am alive and well?" He asked before they said goodbye.

"Got it, Parker," Silvia answered, using his own words.

It was a wonder that anyone was able to deal with his mother without smiling. She was smart, and very quick with words. "Thanks, Mom. I'll talk to you soon."

After hanging up with her son, Silvia sat in her office chair, looking outside. Her husband, Glenn, always said the boys took after her. Both of her sons were handsome, and did have her sense of humor. But, they were both very serious men, and that, they got from their father. It was easy, looking back thirty years, and remembering the silly arguments or differences between her and Glenn. At the time, they seemed monumental, and only time and love were able to keep her and Glenn happily married for this long. She hoped that her sons were able to see the merit of finding someone different than themselves.

Parker hung up with his mother, let Owen know he was now available to take calls, and sat in his office chair staring at a wall. It was not an interesting wall either. It was the wall that held his diplomas and certifications. For some reason, he wondered if Jayde would think his office was boring.

Shaking his head, he returned his attention to the client file he'd been reading earlier.

Jayde's day was busy. She wished it would be busier so she wouldn't think so much about Parker Kinley. Every time the bell on the door chimed, she looked up hoping it was him. And then, every time she realized it wasn't him, she felt a deep disappointment. And then she had to snap herself out of that. It was exhausting.

During her afternoon break, Jayde went for a walk down the street. The weather was hot, as usual for summertime in Galveston. She peeked into the surrounding shops and just strolled along, trying to get some perspective.

"It was one date," She mumbled to herself.

After fifteen minutes of having a losing argument with herself, Jayde pulled out her phone and called Parker. She stood on the sidewalk, nervously waiting for him to pick up.

Parker was between clients and taking a breather when his phone rang. When he saw it was Jayde, he answered quickly, "Hello there."

Jayde couldn't help it, her heart started beating faster. "Hello there yourself. How's your day been going?"

Smiling, Parker told her, "Well, I was counting the minutes until I could call you, but you beat me to it."

"I didn't interrupt you, did I?" Jayde was nervous for a whole different reason now. She didn't want to seem like a creepy stalker type woman.

Getting up to close his office door for privacy, Parker said, "No, not at all." He sat back down at his desk, "I didn't know what kind of breaks you had so I wasn't going to call until after five-thirty."

Appreciating his consideration, Jayde smiled big. "You are a sweet man; did you know that?"

A blush filled Parker's cheeks. He couldn't remember the last time a woman made him blush. Maybe never. "I didn't, but I sure think you're sweet for saying it."

Her pulse speeding up, Jayde thought she might burst. "I know it's a pain for you to come down to the island after work, but I was hoping you could find some time to come down soon." She stopped and thought about her words, before telling him, "Oh, I guess I'm saying things I shouldn't. We never really said we'd have another date."

"A foregone conclusion," Parker told her.

His tone made Jayde's nerves calm, just a little bit. "I'm glad you think so. I was hoping it wasn't just me who had a good time."

She was the sweet one, Parker thought to himself. "After work, I am at your disposal." He announced with a little dramatic flair thrown in.

Before she could think of her words, Jayde teased him with, "You're at my disposal, huh? I guess I'll have to think of something fun for us to do." Once the words were out, Jayde realized how full of innuendo they were. "Uh, you know, out…"

Parker chuckled, "I actually did know that you weren't suggesting anything too intimate." When Jayde didn't answer right away, he added, "But maybe that would be something you'd consider in the future."

With all these words and meanings, Jayde was blushing a bright red. "I get it," She laughed. "Just let me know when you're on your way down, okay?"

"Sure," Parker replied.

They hung up and Jayde took a couple of deep breaths before she went back to the shop. Lord, if a phone call could make her blush like this, what would happen if…. She let the thought trail off, not wanting to open up that particular subject just yet.

Parker finished with his last client a little earlier than expected. He was in Webster, Texas, so he was close to the freeway that he could take down to Galveston. Not even going back to the office, he called Owen, said he was done for the day, and hung up before his shocked assistant started asking too many questions.

Since it was a little earlier that he was on the freeway, traffic wasn't too horrible. There always seemed to be an endless number of cars that were going down to the island. For people in Houston and the surrounding area, this was their fun getaway. Parker was starting to understand the draw himself.

He pulled up in front of Joe's Cuppa Joe at about four forty-five. Sitting in his car, he watched Jayde as she laughed. He wished he could be that carefree with his job. Of course, his job was serious whereas Jayde's allowed for warm conversations and laughter. A bit of jealousy filled his chest but Parker tamped down on it. His life was a good one, and he was proud of the success his business experienced. Parker got out of the car and walked up to the door. As soon as Jayde's eyes met him, he stopped.

Jayde was laughing at Connor's explanation of his prom proposal when she turned her head and her eyes met up with Parker's. It was like someone was reaching into her chest and zapping her heart. Just one look and she was lost in za-za-zing world.

Walking over to the door, she waited for Parker to enter, before she reached over and gave him an impromptu hug. She smiled when she realized how surprised he was. To his credit, he recovered quickly and hugged her back. Without thinking, Jayde kissed the side of his neck and then released him.

Parker wasn't sure what to expect, but Jayde hugging him tightly and then kissing his neck, wasn't even in the realm of his thoughts. Not that he minded. There wasn't anything wrong with being in a beautiful woman's arms. He watched Jayde walk back over to the young man she was talking to. She led him over to where Parker was standing.

"Connor, this is Parker Kinley," Jayde blushed a little because she wasn't sure how to label Parker. "Uh, he's my date."

Giving Parker a look of curiosity, Connor held out his hand to shake Parker's. "Nice to meet you," Connor said quietly.

It wasn't tough for Parker to realize he was being sized up. First by Joe, and now Connor. He was relieved that Jayde had people around who looked out for her. He shook Connor's hand and told him, "Nice to meet you too. Jayde tells me you're a genius."

Connor blushed, and nodded, before replying, "That's what they tell me. And by "they" I mean all my teachers, counselors, and the admission office staff of about fifteen colleges."

There was no gloating in the words so Parker thought that Connor didn't quite understand, or simply didn't care, about being a genius. No slouch himself in his studies, Parker thought it must be tough to be the smartest person in the room. "So, what are you interested in studying?" He asked the teenager.

Jayde watched as Connor and Parker started talking about colleges. She quietly went over and locked the front door, flipping the closed sign over. She let them talk as she started the cleanup process.

Connor suggested they sit down and Parker was very interested in what he had to say. It was a new perspective, hearing such a young person commenting on things. He was certainly impressive and Parker thought it was kind of odd that the kid was working in a coffee shop. He asked Connor, "So, why do you work here?"

Smiling, Connor answered, "It fits the hours that I'm available and, according to my mom, helps me with my social skills."

Biting his lip, Parker just nodded.

"So," Connor started, "You and Jayde are dating?"

He was being checked out, so Parker answered with a confident, "Yes we are."

The kid seemed to contemplate it, and then he said, "Cool."

Parker was pretty sure the "interrogation" was over. He suggested, "If you want to intern for me, for some experience, just give me a call." He handed Connor his business card.

"Hey, thanks," Connor replied. He realized that Jayde was doing all the cleaning up so he gave Parker a smile and then got up to start lifting chairs up off the floor.

Parker stayed where he was and just watched Jayde and Connor as they went through their closing routine. It was easy to see the camaraderie they shared. Jayde would tease the kid about stuff and he would tease her right back. In no time they were yelling, "Bye," to Joe and walking toward the door.

Jayde smiled at Parker and told him, "I'm ready when you are."

The three of them left the shop, and Jayde locked the door behind them so no one would walk in on Joe while he was finishing up the prep for the next day.

Connor waived his goodbye and hopped onto his moped.

Jayde gave Parker a big smile. "Do you mind if I run my bag up to my apartment and then we can go grab a bite to eat?"

"Sure," Connor answered.

They walked over to the door that led up to the apartments and Jayde preceded him inside.

Parker wasn't sure she wanted him to go up to her apartment so he offered, "I'll just wait down here."

Nodding, Jayde answered, "Sure, I'll be right back," and she darted up the stairs.

Parker was standing down in the small entryway looking around. There were four mailboxes and a bike locked up to a bar that was attached to the wall. Everything was very tidy and Parker knew, without any reservations, that Joe kept everything in good shape.

   Jayde opened up her apartment door, dropped her bag, and looked in the small mirror she kept by the front door to check last minute appearances before throwing on a clean t-shirt. She tucked her debit card and keys into the pocket of her shorts. She'd run up the stairs but decided to walk down them. She could see the top of Parker's head over the railing. He was standing there so quietly, and Jayde thought he was so cute.

   As she got down to the last couple of stairs, Parker turned around and gave her a smile. His smile was beautiful and Jayde, not thinking about it, reached out to touch his cheek as she was stepping down to the last step.

   Everything suddenly slowed down. It was like time was stopping, and the look in his eyes matched her own……want.

   Again, Jayde just went with her heart. She leaned forward and kissed Parker softly on the lips.

   Parker wasn't sure what happened. He looked up to see Jayde coming down the stairs, then she was touching his cheek, and then she was kissing him. He was the luckiest son-of-a-gun on the planet. Her lips were warm and soft. They put him in some kind of warm trance and had his body jumping to attention at the same time. What kiss did that? He wasn't sure but he wasn't going to stop her or complain.

Jayde was enjoying Parker's returning kiss. He lifted his hands and lightly placed them on her forearms. She was still on a step above him which basically made them the same height. It also made kissing him more enjoyable because she didn't have to look up for their lips to meet. He was an experienced kisser, and made her feel as though he wanted to explore every millimeter of her lips. She let out a sigh.

There was a loud slam that made them both part quickly. There, in the doorway, was an angry looking Joe.

Joe was tired, and he sure as hell didn't expect to walk through the door to find Jayde kissing that slick CPA guy. He cleared his throat, and mumbled, "There are other places for that."

Without saying anything else, Joe went past them and started up the stairs. As soon as his door closed, Jayde turned to Parker, and gave him a sheepish smile, saying, "I'm sorry."

Chapter 6

As they walked the few blocks to the restaurant, Parker wondered if he'd really screwed up. Not in the kissing Jayde part, but in the ticking off Joe part. The man intimidated him. He was so lost in his thoughts that he didn't notice Jayde stopping in front of him until she touched his arm. He looked up to see her concerned face and smiled. "I'm sorry, I guess I was lost in my thoughts."

Jayde knew what was occupying his thoughts, "Or, I would conclude that you were worried about us getting caught kissing by Joe."

Smiling, Parker nodded. "Well, he is very protective and I don't need to piss him off by kissing you in his hallway."

Not sure if she should be touched that Parker was so worried about Joe's feelings, or frustrated because she was an adult and should be able to kiss who she wanted, Jayde spoke softly. "I think it's evident, Parker, that you are a sensitive man who respects me. But I really enjoyed kissing you so if you're worried about Joe, then maybe we should rethink this dating thing."

Parker was surprised by the statement. Jayde always seemed a little reserved, so hearing her say she enjoyed the kissing, was a complete turn on. "Uh, yes ma'am," He spoke up quickly.

"That's what I thought," Jayde teased him. "Now, I'm hungry. That kiss worked up an appetite."

A whole new feeling was distracting Parker now. She didn't even understand how her words affected him. Without speaking, he just took her hand into his and started walking again.

They ate, and talked, ate, and talked some more. It was completely casual, with comments about their respective days.

Jayde was listening to Parker talk about his assistant, Owen. Her impression was that Parker respected his assistant and only wanted Owen to succeed. Being a product of a great work environment herself, the words only served to endear him more. He was a caring man, something that wasn't as common a quality as it used to be.

"So, do you think Owen will become an Actuary?" Jayde asked.

Silently thinking, Parker finally replied, "I'm not sure. I think it's a bit too boring for him, but you never know."

Leaning forward, Jayde placed her hand over Parker's. "I don't think you're boring at all."

Again, her words were Parker's undoing. "Well," He cleared his throat, "I have to say that since meeting you, I've loosened up a little bit."

Jayde leaned back in her seat, and stared at him. She was thinking of things she really had no business thinking about. They'd only been out a few times but the connection she felt to Parker was something so different and so unexpected. Jayde had a hard time even putting it into perspective.

Watching Jayde, Parker could tell she was mentally elsewhere. "What are you thinking?" He asked quietly.

A slow smile curled Jayde's lips upward. She blushed. "I was just thinking that even though we've only known each other for a few days, I am looking forward to sleeping with you."

Surprise was an understatement. Parker swallowed hard. He didn't expect Jayde to say something like that. Sure, he was feeling a want he hadn't felt before with any woman, but he certainly didn't think Jayde would be so forward with her own thoughts. It was a little intimidating and extremely arousing all at the same time. "Uh," He started to say, not really knowing what he should say.

Still smiling, Jayde put her hand over Parker's and said, "I'm not expecting anything, Parker, it's just that life is way too short. I am very attracted to you and I don't think I want to waste time playing the shy type when I really want to be with you."

It was like Jayde knew he was on fire and decided to just throw gasoline on him to make it more explosive. "I, uh," Parker cleared his throat, "am just surprised."

Now Jayde was embarrassed. She'd spoken out of her feelings. For the first time, she wondered if Parker felt the same thing. "I'm sorry," She rushed. "I guess I thought you felt the same way."

Not waiting for him to answer, Jayde got up to leave. She wanted to hide away from the mortification that engulfed her. She was out of the door and on the sidewalk heading back to her apartment when Parker caught up to her.

"Jayde," Parker said as he followed her down the street. Her words were so honest and so awesome. He was caught off guard, something that seemed to be usual in his time with Jayde. "Wait up," He said, lightly touching her shoulder, and relieved when she stopped and turned around to look at him. He could see unshed tears in her eyes. "Hey," He cupped her chin in his hand. "What's wrong?"

Over the years, Jayde had people tell her that her "filter" was non-existent. She never felt that way, it was just that losing her mother young made her realize that the important things didn't need to be left unsaid. This was the first time she wondered if those people were right.

"I'm just not into playing hard-to-get, Parker." She allowed the tears to run down her cheeks. "I just wanted you to know how I felt."

"And, it's amazing," Parker whispered as he stepped closer. "If I gave you the impression that I didn't find it amazing that you say what's in your mind and in your heart, then I am the one who is apologizing." He smiled as she looked into his eyes, "When you say things like that, then I'm feeling very un-gentlemanly."

It was Jayde's turn to smile now. "Really?" She asked, her eyes pleading with his. "It's just that I'm crazy about you," It took a lot of strength to tell him what was in her heart. "I think about you all the time and that kiss..." Her words trailed off.

"Was amazing," Parker finished her sentence.

Nodding, Jayde really looked at him. His eyes were expressive, and she wondered how she never noticed that before. They were bright, and very intense.

Parker decided to follow Jayde's lead. "I think about you all the time too." He smiled, "And I'm going to kiss you, Jayde."

His eyes changed then, getting darker, and Jayde waited for him to make good on his words. It was like the whole world slowed down as his face lowered toward hers. Then, his lips covered hers, and her heart felt like it was outside of her body, it was beating so hard.

They stood on the sidewalk, kissing.

Joe was up in his apartment when he heard the downstairs door open. He listened for footsteps on the stairs and only opened the door when he was sure there was only one person coming up. Jayde was stepping onto the landing when he came out of his apartment.

"Uh, Jayde," Joe began, his nerves were showing and he didn't appreciate it at all.

Jayde knew that speaking to Joe was inevitable. He was her boss, and her neighbor. She watched him, surprised that he seemed nervous. "Yes, Joe," She answered.

Joe nodded, not comfortable with all this talking stuff. "I guess it was rude of me to comment about your young man."

As far as apologies went, Jayde knew this was the closest she'd get to one from Joe. She decided to let him off the hook. "Listen Joe," She started, "I know that you are very protective, and believe me, I am so Blessed to have that. I know that we're neighbors too, and I probably shouldn't be kissing anyone in the hallway, but you have to cut Parker some slack. I like him a lot."

Not relishing his "dressing down" from Jayde, Joe merely nodded again. "I can see that," He told Jayde, hoping to sound less critical.

"Well then," Jayde suggested, "how about I don't kiss him in the hallway and you refrain from any comments?"

Sighing, Joe answered, "Sure." He nodded again and went back into his apartment.

Jayde felt better as she walked into her apartment a minute later. It was complicated, having so much contact with Joe. It blurred the lines and she never had any problems with those lines before now. Of course, no one like Parker was ever in the picture before. Parker was important and Joe would have to get used to that. She absently scratched Mr. Beethoven's neck and went into her bathroom to change for bed.

Parker made it home from his dinner with Jayde and missed her the whole way. Walking into his empty house felt wrong for some reason. He stood in the middle of his living room and tried to look at it through Jayde's eyes. The place was tasteful but again, he felt it was way too stark. It needed some color for sure.

After he got ready for bed, Parker sat down out on his patio and dialed Jayde's number. He hoped it wasn't too late. She got up early so he didn't have any idea what time she went to bed. He smiled when she answered, saying "Hello."

"Hello," Parker replied, "I wanted to hear your voice again before I went to bed." He was trying to be more open.

Jayde smiled. His sweet words did wonderful things to her heart. "That was sweet," She wanted to be honest. "I miss you already."

It only took a few words from Jayde to make Parker's body go crazy. His pulse sped up, his mind went fuzzy, and he was aware of everything. Her breathing, the sound of her voice, and her words made things so clear in his mind. "I'm glad."

It was easy to say what she felt when it came to Parker. "I wish you'd kissed me again when you walked me home."

Feeling bad for disappointing Jayde, Parker told her, "I was afraid Joe would come down those steps and kick my ass." He was only half-joking.

"Well, Joe and I had a little talk when I came upstairs." Jayde informed him. "There's an agreement, I won't kiss you in the hallway and he won't make comments that put the fear of God into you."

Parker chuckled. The sad part was, Joe did put the fear of God into him. The man clearly looked at himself as Jayde's protector. Parker couldn't shake the feeling that Joe's disapproval wasn't so easily dismissed, but he knew Jayde meant what she said. "That is good news."

Jayde didn't want to talk about Joe anymore. "So," She began, "what about us getting together at your place? You've been sweet to come down here the last couple of days and it's time I return the favor."

A wave of nerves flooded Parker's gut. "Uh, that would be great," He answered, then asked her, "Do you have a car?"

Silly boy, Jayde thought to herself. "I have a plan," She explained. "How about tomorrow, seven o'clock? Just text me your address."

"It's a date," Parker replied. He was already looking around the house, making a mental note about cleaning up the, already immaculate, space.

They spoke for a few more minutes and then hung up.

After speaking to Parker, Jayde felt keyed up. No wonder, she thought to herself, the man was making her body play its own symphony.

There was no way she would get any sleep, so she decided to go downstairs to the shop and get out her Someday book. There were some things she wanted to put in it.

Joe gave her a spare key when she started working at the shop "just in case." She'd never had a reason to use it before now. Putting on her sweater, Jayde went downstairs as quietly as she could. There was no noise coming from Joe's place so she opened the door and walked over to the door leading into the shop.

It was very different coming in the shop when they weren't actually working. It was dark and a little scary. Without turning on lights, Jayde made her way back through the kitchen. There was a small light on the desk with the computer that was lit up so Jayde made quick work of getting her journal.

With the notebook tucked into her sweater, Jayde was almost to the door when she heard a noise from behind her. Then a low voice said, "You'd better be leaving without anything or you're going to have a back full of buckshot."

Jayde's voice was squeaking as she replied, "Joe, it's me, Jayde."

"Jayde," Joe yelled, "what the hell are you doing in here?" He almost shot her!

Wiping her hand down her face, trying to control her heartrate, Jayde told him, "I wanted my notebook," she pulled it out and showed it to him. "I wanted to write some stuff in it."

Mumbling, "Damn notebook," Joe walked over to where Jayde was standing. He took her by the arm and told her, "Let's go."

Jayde walked out of the shop, waited for Joe to lock it up again, and then led the way to the apartments. She felt like a little kid who was doing something bad. But, she really shouldn't since she wasn't. "Joe," She turned to him before he went into his apartment. "You gave me a key and I needed something personal."

"Yeah, a notebook," Joe retorted. "It's fine, Jayde. I just wished you would have told me. Next time just send me one of those text messages you kids are so fond of these days."

She couldn't help it, she smiled. "Yes, sir," She replied and then gave him a short wave before continuing up to her own apartment.

Once Jayde was inside her place, she picked up Mr. Beethoven and began rubbing his back. He purred out of delight and Jayde waited until the rhythmic motion of petting him calmed her frayed nerves.

She certainly didn't want to upset Joe a second time this evening. She was trying to be respectful and not bother him. After putting down Mr. Beethoven, Jayde took out her notebook and cuddled up on the small loveseat she used in her "living room."

Even though her intention was to write something in the Someday book, Jayde found herself leafing through the pages. She giggled at some of the silly things she wrote down. Learning to ice skate probably wasn't going to happen here in Galveston. Neither would making a snowman. Other things were more practical. She'd even completed a few of the things she wrote ages ago, so that was good. Finishing high school, starting college were a few of the things she could "cross off" her list. Two things caught Jayde's attention. The first was that she would put down, meet my dad or find my dad, every few years. The other one was an entry she made when she was about fifteen, if the handwriting was right. It said, meet a handsome man. Taking out a pen, Jayde said aloud, "Consider this completed." Then she smiled.

The next morning, Jayde was a little nervous about seeing Joe. She hoped he didn't harbor any residual grumpiness from the day before. If his quick nod hello was any indication, he was acting his usual grumpy self today. That was something that Jayde understood and was used to.

As Joe was prepping the kitchen for his baked goods, Jayde took her Someday book and put it in the drawer of the desk. When she turned around, she found Joe was looking at her. "Yes, Joe?" She asked him with a smile.

"What's so important about that notebook?" Joe asked her.

Knowing it probably sounded ridiculous, Jayde shored up her resolve and spit out, "It's my Someday book. It holds all my dreams, big and small."

Joe seemed to consider her answer, then he nodded and went back to making his muffins.

They opened the shop on time and Jayde was thrown into the weekend traffic coming in and out.

Saturdays were crazy and she only worked until 2pm. Normally, if it was busy, she would just stay until closing. That's why she told Parker they would meet at seven o'clock, in case she was staying. She didn't want to leave Joe in a lurch.

As she was bussing a table, Joe was at the counter checking out another customer. He was cordial but Jayde would never say he exuded warmth. It made her wonder why he wanted to run this kind of business. But, after reading her dreams in her Someday book, Jayde couldn't fault him for having a dream, even if the dream seemed out of the ordinary for him.

When Jayde came back behind the counter, Joe asked her, "So what kind of things do you put in this notebook of yours?"

She thought that Joe was acting out of character by asking the question, but she was honest, and replied, "Some of it is really silly but some of it is serious." She smiled at customers who just walked in. "I have find my dad in there, but I also have build a snowman in there." She smiled at Joe before grabbing her order pad, "It's just filled with things I really want to do in my life."

Joe watched Jayde as she greeted the customers who just sat down. She was perky and personable and that's why Joe was so thankful for her and the work she did here at the shop. He knew, deep down, that this wasn't a forever thing for her. She probably had bigger dreams, like she listed in her little notebook, so he'd just support her as best he could.

Although she was busy, Jayde still found time to wonder why Joe asked questions about her Someday book. It was very strange that he showed interest, but it was something she did practically break into the shop to get, so he probably figured it was important.

At two in the afternoon, Joe shouted, "Jayde, aren't you leaving?"

Looking at her phone, Jayde smiled, "I am if you say I can go."

Giving Jayde a stern look, Joe said, "Go!"

Jayde kissed Connor on the cheek, smiling when he blushed, and undid her apron.

She made it upstairs in just minutes, typing a quick text to her friend, Felicia. She hoped that Felicia would be okay with her request.

A few minutes later, Felicia texted back saying,

My car is yours to use

Jayde smiled and started to get ready for her dinner date with Parker.

Chapter 7

After making arrangements with Felicia to use her car, Jayde plugged Parker's address into her phone. She knew how to drive, but didn't do it often so it took a few minutes for her to be comfortable.

The traffic getting off the island was awful, so Jayde was happy that she decided to leave early.

Not being off the island that much, Jayde felt a little nervous. She certainly wasn't sheltered, but kept her life pretty insulated. It was her choice to do so and it was a wonderful life. There were times, like now, that made Jayde reconsider things. Should she try to do something "bigger" with her life. So far, her life was what she hoped it would be. Thoughts of her mother popped into her mind, and Jayde allowed them to lull her during the drive. Her mom would have been proud of her because she followed her heart. That was something her mother always said, "Follow your heart." Jayde smiled, knowing that she was doing that right now too, in going to see Parker.

It was easy to get distracted by Parker. Not just his looks, but his whole being was distracting, but in a totally awesome way. Jayde found herself thinking of him at moments when she least expected it. Having such a connection to someone in such a short period of time was extremely unsettling. He brought out a complex mix of excitement and nervousness in Jayde, and that was just when he looked at her. That kiss….well, that was a whole other matter. Jayde now understood why the women in movies practically swooned when those handsome men kissed them.

Parker arrived home a little early. He'd gone to work this morning, excited for the day to finish up so he could get home. About halfway through the morning, the doubts crept in. He was proud of his life, his home, and everything he'd accomplished, so he couldn't understand why he was so nervous about Jayde seeing his house.

Even Owen knew something was up. Before lunch, his assistant came into the office and told him, "If you don't calm down, I'm going to have to fire you."

The comment was enough to make Parker stop. He was usually quite analytical about these things, but with Jayde, the whole thing changed. After giving Owen the appropriate look of apology, Parker managed to get to work and the rest of the day flew by.

Now that he was home, he wondered about everything. Was his choice for dinner okay? Did he have some clothes that didn't look like he was headed to the office? Were the throw pillows on the sofa too dull looking? "Stop it!" He finally yelled at no one.

Jayde pulled into the driveway of Parker's house almost a half hour early. She was excited to see him but didn't want to put him out. After shutting off the car, she looked up to see him standing in the front doorway. With a little wave, she got out of the car.

As he walked over to her, Jayde told him, "I'm sorry I'm so early."

Parker smiled, and told her, "I get more time with you," before taking her into his arms and kissing her.

The kiss, like the one the night before, was sweet. And it rocked them both.

Jayde found herself folded into Parker's arms and was in Heaven. His lips were so soft and allowed her to take the lead. She wrapped her arms around his waist and held on for dear life.

When they parted, Jayde kept her arms around Parker. "Thank you for that welcome," She teased him. When he blushed, she said, "And thanks for agreeing to this date at your place."

"I'm a pretty smart guy," Parker replied. "When a beautiful woman says she's coming over to my place for dinner, I agree." He winked at her and leaned forward for another quick kiss before releasing her.

They walked, arm and arm, up to the house. Jayde looked around and smiled. The house was beautifully landscaped. She could tell that Parker took pride in his home.

When they walked through the front door, Parker offered to take Jayde's purse. She handed it to him with a smile, as she looked around his home. Being here, she hoped, would give her some insight into Parker's life.

Parker watched Jayde as she looked around. The house was an open concept so you could see the kitchen, dining room, and living room from the front door. His real estate agent assured him it was great for entertaining, but Parker never entertained. "I'm pretty nervous about you seeing my house," He confessed.

A look of surprise crossed Jayde's face. "Really?" She asked him. "I was super excited to see it. I'm hoping it gives me some fascinating insight into you."

Still holding Jayde's hand, he squeezed it gently, then asked her, "What kind of insights?"

Allowing him to lead her, Jayde followed him down a couple of stairs and into the living room. It was large, with a sectional on one side, and accent chairs on the other. The room was designed for conversations. "Well," She started, "I guess it's just seeing you at home, what kind of things do you like? I wonder about what you do here at night."

Her words gave Parker pause. "Well," He turned to her and brought her hand up to his lips. "I had this place professionally decorated so it wasn't really my taste." He looked around, as if trying to see it through her eyes, "but it's a place I lay my head in. I read a lot, mostly reports from work." He led her over to the sofa and motioned for her to sit before joining her. "I think it's okay," He paused, "but it's just my house."

It was a shame that Parker didn't seem to understand how lucky he was. "A home is important, Parker, it's where we can be totally free to be ourselves, whoever that may be."

A wise comment, Parker thought. "And what do you do in your home?" He asked Jayde.

It took a moment of consideration before Jayde answered him. She was a little embarrassed. "Mostly," She told him, "I do meditation, I pet my cat, Mr. Beethoven, and I read too. Only I read history books, self-help books, basically anything that I find interesting."

Parker could picture her, cuddled up in a chair, her cat beside her, reading a book. It was a sweet picture that did crazy things to his insides. It made him warm and he smiled at the thought.

Jayde saw him smile, and asked, "What's that look for?"

Parker's smile widened. "I was just thinking of you, sitting in an oversized chair, petting your cat, and totally engrossed in a book. It made me smile."

"Parker," Jayde whispered, trying to get the words around the emotions she was feeling, "I am constantly surprised at how your words make me feel."

Sitting back, Parker studied her. Emotion lined her features, but gave her a beauty that no one could ever force. "I am constantly surprised at how everything you do makes me feel," He replied.

The conversation was quickly changing, at least in Jayde's mind. There was a light-hearted tone, but the words ran deep. "Parker, I'm not a woman who plays games. I just don't know how, and I wouldn't even if I did. Life is too short for that crap." She rubbed her thumb across his hand, enjoying the delightful awareness the touch caused. "I'm here because it's what I want. I just want you to tell me if we're on the same page. If we're not, no harm done."

Never, in all the time he'd been around women, had Parker ever understood one. Jayde changed all of that. "I can't even tell you how much your honesty means. I'm not a game-player either. I'm a busy guy who loves his job, loves his family, and tries to do the right thing." He searched her eyes for a few moments, and continued, "I'm in completely new territory with you and I think it's exciting and damn scary at the same time."

Jayde giggled. "I'm relieved that you feel the same way I do."

Looking at her intently, Parker asked, "I never thought I would find someone who seems so different, but understands me."

"How do you think we're different?" Jayde asked, curious.

Considering his thoughts, Parker wanted to be clear. "Well, you're very full of life and you are so open." He sighed, "I'm really uptight, I guess, in comparison. My job is pretty serious so I am too."

Jayde threw her head back and laughed. "I'm not laughing at you, just that you consider yourself so uptight." Her eyes still alive with humor, she told him, "I think you're a very decent man, an honorable man."

"I think someone is getting a little off track," Parker teased, trying to get his feelings under control. If they stayed on this path, he wasn't sure he could keep from kissing Jayde.

It was so easy to laugh with him, Jayde thought to herself. "I'm not off track, I'll have you know. I'm downright certifiable."

Tapping Jayde on the nose with his finger, Parker told her, "And it's incredibly sexy."

Again, the atmosphere changed. It was charged with electricity that was running between them. Jayde knew Parker felt it too. His eyes were getting darker and his breath shallowed.

His reaction made her brave, so Jayde asked, "Parker, I'd really like it if you kissed me."

"I think I'd like that too," Parker mumbled as he pulled her closer to him.

This time, the kiss wasn't chaste, it wasn't even in the same universe. This kiss was heat, mingled breaths, sighs, and pure need.

Jayde found her hands had a mind of their own, wandering up Parker's arms, diving into his hair, grabbing on for dear life as he swept her up into the atmosphere with his kisses.

Moments, or minutes, later; Parker wasn't sure which, they parted enough so they could each catch their breath.

Parker watched Jayde absently rubbing her hands down her sides, as if she were trying to straighten herself out in some way. He was pretty sure that if someone walked in right now, they would know what was going on. The funny thing was, even with just kissing, Parker felt closer to Jayde than he had to any other woman. If this was what was happening after only a few days, he wondered how quickly it would take him to fall all the way. And he was most definitely falling.

Jayde was embarrassed and didn't even understand why she felt that way. The kisses were great, amazing, practically earth-shattering. So why was she scared and worried that she didn't measure up in some way? "Why don't we work on dinner?" She suggested, trying to give herself a minute.

They got up and went into the kitchen. Parker had a roast going in a slow cooker. He pulled the lid up and smiled as the aroma drifted into the room. "I think it's about ready," He told Jayde.

They set the table together, as if they'd been doing it for ages.

Parker took his time getting their plates dished up with food. He wanted to make a great impression with Jayde. "I hope you like it," He grinned as he put the plates down onto the table.

"I'm sure it's great," Jayde returned. She took a bite, and her eyes grew wide. "It's wonderful, Parker."

It was impossible not to feel good when a woman was happy with something you cooked, "I'm glad you like it. My mom spent years trying to get my brother and I to basically not suck at cooking."

Chuckling, Jayde took her time savoring the meal. "Well, you've done her proud."

"I'll pass that on," Parker smiled, "I'm sure she'll then begin the interrogation about you."

His words almost caused Jayde to choke. Panic welled up into her throat. "Me?" She asked, a frightened look on her face.

Intrigued by her reaction to his mother's questions gave Parker pause. Clearly, Jayde didn't realize how wonderful she was. He sensed there were some issues that Jayde may have in regards to how others viewed her. "I'll be sure to tell her all about your wonderful qualities," He tried to reassure her.

"What will she ask?" Jayde asked, very curious.

Sighing, Parker ran through the "checklist" in his mind, before answering with, "Well, she'll ask about how we met, what you look like, what your job is, and probably about twenty other questions I haven't even thought of."

The panic was taking on a whole new level in Jayde's stomach. She couldn't eat anymore because her stomach was now in knots. "Oh, well maybe you shouldn't tell her just yet."

Parker leaned back in his chair. "Can I ask why?" He inquired.

Jayde felt silly and embarrassed but having Parker's mother asking about her was really scary. She had no choice but to be honest. "Well, I'm not sure we've been seeing each other long enough to start talking about it."

He didn't buy her reasoning, and told her, "You didn't seem to have any problems saying something to Joe," he asked, "Are you embarrassed of me?"

Throwing down her napkin, Jayde skirted her chair back and excused herself. When she arrived, Parker told her where the restroom was so she made a mad dash for it. She just needed a minute to breathe.

After shutting the door, Jayde turned into the tiny room. She leaned against the vanity, looking at herself in the mirror. She was ashamed of her behavior. That being said, it didn't change the fact that she was pretty sure Parker's parents wouldn't approve of him dating a barista with barely one year of college under her belt.

She was still standing there when she heard a light knock on the door. Parker asked, "Jayde are you okay?"

"I'll be right out," She tried to answer brightly.

When she came out, her cheeks were flushed. She cleared her throat, and explained, "I'm sorry, I think I had a bit of a panic attack."

Parker nodded. "I could see that. Is it that scary, having my mom know about us?"

"Yes," Jayde rushed out the answer. "It's just, I'm who I am, and you're who you are."

He was getting frustrated. "And that is what?" He asked.

Looking down at her hands, Jayde was even more embarrassed. "Okay, so I think that you're an educated, handsome, great guy, and I'm just a barista with minimal college experience."

Parker took her hands and led her back into the living room. He motioned for her to sit, and then joined her on the sofa. "First of all, I'm not sure whether to be flattered that you actually think any of that means anything, or insulted that you would even consider my family snobby enough to care."

A whole new kind of embarrassment filled Jayde's belly. "I'm so sorry, Parker," She was trying not to cry. "It's just that I've always been happy with who I am, until I start comparing myself to others."

"Why would you? Compare yourself to others?" Parker knew that was the case, but he wanted Jayde to work it out.

Jayde looked up into his eyes, "Not normally, but it matters to me to be good enough for you."

And that one sentence settled everything. "Oh, sweet Jayde," Parker cupped her chin in his hand, "You are probably too good for me, but I'm glad you gave me a chance."

It was tough to keep him at a distance when all he did was make her feel special. Not that she wanted to anyway, but her insecurities seemed to overwhelm her. "Let's agree to disagree on this particular subject," She teased Parker.

"Okay," Parker answered, "As long as I get to kiss you some more."

Her cheeks flushed for a whole different reason, and it made Jayde smile. "I sure hope so."

Chapter 8

The dinner was kind of a hurdle, in Jayde's mind. It was the first test of her own feelings and she was glad that she and Parker could be honest about their thoughts and concerns.

Even the next morning, she sat in bed and went over every second in her mind. They finished dinner and sat out on the patio talking for hours. She didn't want to come back home but Parker didn't ask her to stay and she didn't feel right about inviting herself. It was early in their relationship but Jayde felt like she knew him better than anyone else.

As she looked over at her clock, Jayde realized she still had time to get to church.

An hour later, singing hymns during the service, Jayde's thoughts jumped to Parker. Did he go to church? Did he have a particular faith?

So wrapped up in her thoughts, Jayde didn't even notice when the service ended and people were filing out. She only came out of her mind haze when Sister Marjorie sat down beside her. A flush covered Jayde's cheeks, and she gave a mumbled, "Sorry," to the Sister.

"Why are you sorry?" Sister Marjorie asked. "What better place for reflection than here?"

Jayde was pretty sure that this kind of reflection wasn't what the Priest and congregation had in mind. "I was thinking about Parker." She admitted to the Sister.

A smile on her lips, Sister Marjorie turned toward Jayde. Like a giddy school girl, she asked, "Is that the handsome man that came into the shop?"

Nodding, Jayde couldn't help but smile. "Yes," She confirmed, "we had dinner at his place last night and," Jayde let the words trail off.

"And, you would rather be with him there than here with us?" Sister Marjorie asked plainly.

That wasn't exactly what Jayde was thinking, but it was close enough that it gave her pause. "Not sure about that," She took the Sister's hand and squeezed it, "I'll get back to you."

Growing serious, Sister Marjorie looked around to make sure they were alone, and then began speaking. "I had a conversation with your mother a few weeks before her passing." She squeezed Jayde's hand reassuringly, and continued, "She was upset with me over my religious tutoring to you and she didn't want you to be let down when, as she put it, God didn't answer your prayers."

Since Jayde never knew about this particular conversation, she was intrigued.

Sister Marjorie went on to say, "And I assured her that I would never be too preachy about the Almighty." She smiled, "But I also told her that you would most likely find someone who loved you as much as God did."

"What did she say to that?" Jayde asked her.

Trying to hold back tears, Sister Marjorie replied, "She said that if you found someone who loved you so much, that you should never let them go. I was told to make you see how important love could be." She gave Jayde a quick hug. "Her biggest regret was not finding your father again."

The Sister's statement made Jayde frown. "What do you mean, find my father again?" She asked.

Sister Marjorie leaned back in the pew, said a quick prayer for clarity, and then explained, "That's why she moved you here. Galveston is where your father is from."

This information was a lot for Jayde to process. "Why didn't I ever know about this?" She asked the Sister.

"I can't say why your mother didn't tell you this, I can only tell you about the conversation we had." Sister Marjorie hoped this helped her young friend. "I see the signs of love in your eyes, love for this Parker." She smiled, "And I'm here if you need me."

After nodding to Sister Marjorie, Jayde stayed where she was for a few minutes longer. Her father was from Galveston? Why wouldn't her mother give her that information? If he was from Galveston, why couldn't she find out more about him? The revelation actually left Jayde with more questions than answers.

On the way home, Jayde fought different feelings. She was upset that she didn't know this before. She was sad that her mother thought that God would let her down. And most especially, she was worried about Sister Marjorie telling her she was falling in love with Parker Kinley. They'd known one another for less than a week, and that wasn't nearly long enough for her to know whether it was love or not. As she waited for the light on Broadway Avenue to change, Jayde's mind drifted back.

"Mommy," Jayde asked her mother as they waited for the bus. "Did you love my father?"

Fran gave her daughter a caring look with a hint of a smile. "Oh yes, Jayde," She answered. "I loved him very much."

"Then how come he didn't stay with us?" Jayde asked. She was eight years old now, and she wanted to know why other kids had their daddies and she didn't have hers.

Smiling, Fran answered, "I met him at the beach in California. He was there with friends he worked with and they were playing volleyball. I was walking by with a girlfriend and they asked us to play." The bus arrived, so she helped Jayde up and into a seat, and then continued, "He was so handsome and we just smiled a lot at each other." She looked off dreamily, "And that night, he asked if he could see me again." Holding her daughter's hand, Fran hoped she would look at her father as a good man. "We spent every day together for a month and then he had to go away for work."

Jayde still wanted to know, "So why didn't he come back to us?"

Fran's smile faded, "Well, he had to go out of the country for work and I didn't get a chance to give him my address, or get his before he left." She swiped a tear from her eye, "He didn't know about you or I know he would've stayed with us."

Jayde was jolted back to the present and continued on her ride home. She was almost to the café when she realized she was crying.

Missing her mother was painful enough, but remembering all the what-ifs she missed with her father seemed almost unbearable at times. Of course, the man never even knew about her so he had no idea she even existed and had no idea she was looking for him.

Now Parker, and all the feelings rolling around her heart for him, were mixing everything up even more.

By the time she got her bike inside and locked up, Jayde was wiping away more tears. She hadn't noticed Joe was standing outside his apartment until she almost ran into him. "Oh," She said with a start, "I'm sorry Joe, I must have been daydreaming."

Joe knew that Jayde was upset. She'd come home kind of late the night before, not that he was prying, but he heard her come in. He knew she'd gone to church this morning and he was going to offer to take her to lunch today when he noticed she was crying. "What's wrong?" He ground out the question.

"Oh nothing," Jayde tried to play it off as nothing. "I just found out something about my mom that I hadn't known before. It's not bad, just kind of sad." She smiled, trying to reassure him.

Nodding, Joe told her, "Well, I'm glad it wasn't that fella that you've been seeing," he grimaced, "I'd hate to have to talk to him."

Not expecting his words, Jayde laughed. "Joe, you're a sweetheart," She said, and kissed him on the cheek. "If he gives me any trouble, I'll be sure to tell you first."

"You do that," Joe told her as she continued upstairs. He'd just ask her to lunch some other time.

Sundays were their day off. Joe knew that he could make a lot of money on Sundays but he said that his "daddy would tan his hide if he worked on the Lord's day." And although Jayde never saw Joe go to church, she believed that he had a pretty good relationship with God.

Her phone started ringing as she walked into her apartment. "Hello," She said before checking the caller I.D.

"Hello there," Parker told Jayde. He didn't know if she slept in on the weekends so he deliberately waited until almost noon to call her. With the hours she worked during the week, he thought that it would be crappy if he woke her up needlessly. "Are you up and at em?" He asked with a smile.

Just hearing his voice made Jayde smile. "I have been for about two hours," She answered, then asked him, "What are you up to?"

Parker was standing on his back patio, where they sat the night before. He was remembering their talk and missing her. Seeing Jayde was becoming a necessity. "I'm thinking of you," He stated, just putting the words out there.

"Really?" Jayde asked. He could just say a few words and her heart started tromping around inside her chest.

Chuckling, Parker replied, "Oh yes, really." He walked inside the house, "I think about you a lot. I was sad when you left last night."

All of Jayde's earlier questions were finding answers. "I didn't want to leave," She admitted.

Now all of Parker's insides were in an uproar. "I didn't want you to leave, but I also don't want to be one of those guys."

"What guys?" She asked, baiting him.

Sitting down in a chair, Parker cleared his throat, and told her, "You know, one of those guys who think about one thing and then does whatever it takes to get that one thing."

For someone so polished, Jayde thought he sounded a little prudish. "Parker, are you afraid to tell me that you want me?" She asked.

"No!" He rushed his answer out. "I want you, Jayde," He confessed, "it's just that I don't want you to think that's the only thing I want from you."

Wanting to tease him a little, Jayde asked, "And what if that's all I want from you?"

Growing uncomfortably aroused, Parker swallowed hard, and answered, "Well, I think I'm more than just a booty call, but I'm at your disposal."

Laughing, Jayde replied, "Good to know." She thought he was just so much more than just a simple crush. Although she didn't feel brave enough to give voice to what Sister Marjorie told her earlier, she would spend as much time with Parker as he wanted. She deserved that at least. "Well, do you want to get together today?" She asked him.

"Yes," He answered.

They decided to meet at the shop, and see what they could discover on the island from there.

Jayde snuggled up on the chair and smiled. Just thinking about Parker gave her warm, fuzzy feelings. It was like being a kid on Christmas morning or your birthday; when you just knew a wonderful surprise was coming. The feelings were unlike anything she felt before and although they scared her, it was the very best kind of fear.

Knowing that a lot of times, Joe took Sundays to work on new recipes, Jayde wandered downstairs. She knocked on his door and waited. When he answered, she smiled, and asked, "Got anything new in the works?"

He never smiled, but Jayde made him come damn close. Joe invited her in and motioned for her to sit at the kitchen table. He placed some muffins on a plate and set them down in front of her. "What's on your agenda today?" He asked.

"I'm waiting for Parker and then we'll go exploring," Jayde answered. "I looked at the things going on today and there are a few choices."

Nodding, Joe mentioned, "Give Parker my number and I'll give him some suggestions."

The comment, so out-of-character for Joe, really made Jayde stop. She was midway to taking a bite of a muffin, and had to put it down. "Uh," Jayde stumbled, "Joe you don't seem to like Parker and now you want me to give him your number?"

Even though he knew this would be tough, Joe continued on. "Yes, I want to show you that I respect you and your decisions."

Okay, now Joe was starting to sound like a therapist. "Okkaayy," Jayde drew out the word. "I'll be sure to do that."

After she did finish the muffin, and grabbed a few more for later, Jayde went downstairs to wait for Parker. She did as Joe asked and texted Parker Joe's phone number. Since they were texting, it was difficult to tell if Parker was as confused as she was with Joe's new attitude.

Not wanting to borrow any negative thoughts, Jayde decided to just focus on finding something for them to do on the island. She was still looking at her phone when Parker pulled up a little while later.

"Hello there," Parker greeted her as he jumped out of the driver's side to come around the car. She was beautiful, her smile big and her eyes soft.

Jayde walked over to meet him as he stepped up onto the curb. She wrapped her arms around his neck and reached up to kiss him. It was easy now, she appreciated the comfort of feeling free to express herself with Parker. "Hello yourself," She responded when she released his lips from her own.

Smiling, Parker opened up the car door, and asked her, "Are you ready?"

Planting a big smile on her lips, Jayde nodded, and replied, "You bet," as she got into the car.

When she got into the car, Jayde saw the handful of flowers sitting on the center console of the car. "What are these?" She asked as Parker got into the car.

"For you," Parker answered, he waited to start up the car, turning to Jayde and saying, "my neighbor has this huge garden that's just beautiful, and I asked if I could pick some of her flowers."

The thought of him doing that made Jayde's chest swell with emotion. "Really?" She asked, tears of happiness threatening.

Just seeing that smile on Jayde's face made Parker's day. Never did he ever think that a woman's smile could make so much difference in his day. That was pretty amazing. "Yes, really," He whispered before leaning in and giving Jayde one more kiss. Reluctantly pulling away, he started up the car.

Since it was Sunday, the traffic was a little hectic.

Jayde looked out the window, just enjoying being with Parker.

Every chance he got, Parker would look over and watch Jayde. She was quiet, but he thought she looked very happy. "You're looking thoughtful," He commented as they waited at a traffic light.

"I'm just content," Jayde told him, smiling. "It's easy with you," She explained.

Her words just turned him inside out. "It's easy with you too," Parker reciprocated. "So, I have this plan."

Jayde shot him a playful look, "That you're not going to tell me about."

Frowning, Parker asked, "How did you know I was going to say that?"

Stifling a giggle, Jayde answered, "Because I work around people all day almost every day and I recognize the "I've got a secret" look."

Parker laughed. She was never dull. "Okay then," He nodded and started to drive again when the light turned green.

They were headed down to the east end of the island so Jayde wondered if they were going to take the Ferry. It was kind of exciting since Jayde always wanted to take the Ferry over to Bolivar but just never got around to it. Surprisingly though, Parker turned off toward the East Beach so she had to change her way of thinking.

Parker watched Jayde and her questioning eyes. If surprising her could be this fun, he'd be sure to do it again. "Almost there," He commented.

A few minutes later, he pulled onto the public beach. Parker didn't even know this beach existed since he'd only been to the West Beach here on the island. When he found out about this one, he knew he had to bring Jayde.

"So, we're walking on the beach," Jayde commented as she got out of the vehicle.

Parker laughed. "Sort of," He told her. He came around the vehicle and took Jayde's hand into his.

They weren't going toward the water, which surprised Jayde. She saw a few other buildings around but didn't know what was up. Only when they got closer to the buildings did she notice what was ahead of them. "Horses," She shouted in happiness. She loved horses! They were majestic animals that always seemed so intense. Strong, vibrant, and she imagined riding on the back of one someday.

A young woman came out to meet them, and asked, "Are you Mr. Kinley?"

Parker nodded yes.

"I'm Donna," She introduced herself, then told them, "this way please."

Giving Parker a questioning look, Jayde followed the woman silently.

They walked around the fence and came face-to-face with two horses.

Jayde couldn't help it, she made a small squeak of pleasure. "They're gorgeous," She said with quiet excitement.

She reached forward and offered her hand to the first horse. He was tall and broad, with a brownish red colored coat. "Aren't you beautiful," She purred to the horse.

Parker watched in fascination as the horse took in Jayde's compliment with the same enthusiasm that he, himself, had when Jayde showed him affection. He guessed that even horses weren't immune to beautiful ladies. "I looked up some activities and found this," He put his hand on Jayde's back, and whispered, "we're going horseback riding on the beach."

If Jayde was excited about seeing the horses, the prospect of riding them was making her heart fly through the roof. "Are you kidding me?" She asked Parker, with all the excitement of a young child.

"Nope," Parker answered, "Let's do this."

Chapter 9

Within minutes they were each introduced to a horse, and got into the saddles.

The tour guide led them onto the beach and they were going at a leisurely pace. The wind off the Gulf was blowing wildly and Jayde was glad she pulled her hair back before they left her place.

Parker was just behind Jayde as they were guided down the beach. There was something very peaceful in the way the leather saddle made noise with each step the horse took. He was on a tan Palomino named Fred. The simple name clearly did not fit the animal, who was an example of repressed power. Parker would bet his last dollar that this horse was one who liked to run. Hearing Jayde's voice, Parker snapped out of his thoughts.

Wanting to enjoy this time with Parker, Jayde slowed down the pace of her horse so Parker could be side-by-side with her. He was in a mental zone and seemed to come out of it when she said, "Thank you," to him.

Seeing the pleasure on Jayde's face made Parker happy. She looked free, her hair blowing in the breeze, atop a beautiful horse. "For what?" He asked her.

Jayde gave Parker a skeptical look. "For what?" She repeated back, "For doing this."

Laughing, Parker replied, "It was my pleasure."

Their guide, Donna, motioned for them to come up beside her. They listened as she talked about the bird/turtle sanctuary on this side of the island.

About thirty minutes into the ride, Donna asked if they wanted to get some pictures with the horses. Parker handed her his phone and they moved their horses closer so they could lean toward one another. Donna took the pictures and smiled.

Jayde asked, "Do you mind if we get down and stand in front of the horses?"

Donna nodded yes, and waited for them to dismount.

With the horses flanking them, both Jayde and Parker stood next to one another. With one hand loosely holding the horse's reins, Jayde snuggled into Parker's side. She couldn't remember the last time she was this blissfully happy. Donna snapped a few more pictures. When Jayde thought she was done, she looked up at Parker and said, "You are so very sweet, Parker Kinley."

Parker heard Jayde's words and his heart flipped. He looked down at her, and said, "As long as you look this happy, I'll do whatever you want, Jayde."

Forgetting that Donna was watching, Jayde lifted her hand and placed it on Parker's chest. His heart was beating as fast as her own. Her eyes linked with his and there was this monumental shift inside of her. "Kiss me," She murmured.

A smile on his lips, Parker leaned toward her, and softly said, "My pleasure."

Donna kept snapping pictures on the phone as the two kissed. She almost felt bad about witnessing this personal moment, but it was a magical thing, watching people fall in love.

As if they remembered that Donna was there, both Jayde and Parker ended their kiss.

Parker gave her a boost up into her saddle and she waited as he got up onto his own horse before they continued on the ride.

Donna was kind enough to give him back his phone so Parker was able to snap candid pictures of Jayde, the Gulf of Mexico, and the horses. He was pretty sure this was something neither he nor Jayde would forget any time soon.

At the end of the guided tour, one of the assistants took their horses away. Parker suggested, "Jayde, why don't you go and visit with the horses while I finish up with Donna."

Jayde happily walked over to where the horses were standing in the paddock.

Donna smiled at Parker while he took care of paying for their rides. "I half thought you were going to propose," She commented casually. It happened more than people thought.

Shocked by the guide's words, Parker asked, "Why?"

Working with horses, and people, as much as she did, Donna could spot love pretty quick. "I don't see that many people who are as in love as the two of you are."

Hearing a stranger make that kind of assumption made Parker pause. "Uh," He tried to figure out words that wouldn't make him sound like a jerk. "Not quite there yet," He told Donna, and then thanked her again for the great experience.

As he was walking over to where Jayde was standing, gently petting the nuzzle of the horse, and speaking softly, his heart did another flip. Just looking at this woman made him want to take chances with his heart. That was something he never thought he would want to do.

Fear began to creep into his mind, and Parker thought maybe he just needed some space. This relationship was going pretty fast and it was scaring the hell out of him. "Hey," He said to Jayde as he came up beside her.

"Thank you, Parker," Jayde looked over at him. "This was amazing."

Any fear that Parker thought he felt, only moments ago, dissipated. "I'm glad you liked it." He looked down the beach, and then asked her, "Do you want some lunch?"

"I'd love it," Jayde replied. With one last scratch of the horse's mane, she walked toward his car. "What do you feel like eating?" She asked Parker.

Knowing that he couldn't say what was going through his mind, Parker pretended to be deep in thought. "I don't know, how about we just walk down the Seawall and see what draws us in."

Smiling, Jayde nodded, "Sounds good."

After tucking her into the passenger seat, Parker walked around to get into the car. He wasn't sure how to handle these see-saw emotions he was having around Jayde.

The rest of the afternoon was spent walking down the seawall and poking around every shop they came across. Most of them were souvenir shops but Jayde insisted they walk around, just in case. She told Parker that, "You never know when you'll uncover a treasure."

That take on things really had his mind going. She had such an openness about her. She took things in and just mentally allowed them to absorb into her being. Parker never had that particular gift and he was in awe of how easy Jayde made things seem.

They were walking along the beach, after lunch, and Jayde stopped. She just looked up at the sky and Parker looked up too, but couldn't figure out what she was so interested in. Finally, he asked her, "What do you see?"

Pointing upward, Jayde told him, "You see how those clouds just sort of streak across the sky, well, I think that's God using a paintbrush to give us something magical to look at."

Parker looked up again, and could see exactly what Jayde was saying. "I never thought of it that way," He said.

"Most people don't," Jayde said as she looked at him. "My mother always said I had an eye for things that others didn't see." They began walking along the beach again, with Jayde bending down to pick up seashells here and there. "It was fine when I was a kid, but during high school, it was a nightmare." She tried to contain the hurt and rejection she was given from other teenagers. "I was pretty much picked on all through school."

Not imagining that was possible, Parker said, "No way."

Jayde nodded, and returned, "Way."

"I'm sorry," He said, and reached over to take Jayde's hand. "Teenagers are real jerks."

With a half chuckle, Jayde replied, "Well, they certainly aren't known for their warm and fuzzy selves," she smiled when he laughed. "But I had a couple of great friends, like Felicia, who stuck with me."

For some reason, Parker felt angry towards people he never met and probably would never meet. He thought it was really crappy for kids to treat such a good person like Jayde so badly. "Well, I'm glad you didn't change because of those jackasses!"

Hearing the emotion and anger in Parker's words forced Jayde to stop walking. She loved the protective edge she heard. "I'm no worse for the wear, Parker, and, if anything, it reinforced my resolve to be exactly who I was."

"Good to hear," Parker told her.

They walked further down the beach and Parker asked, "So did you walk the Seawall for a week straight?"

Sighing, Jayde answered, "Well, I started to but then this really handsome guy came into the shop and swept me off my feet." She was over exaggerating the words, and was glad that Parker was smiling. It was the truth but she wasn't sure that she was ready to be that open with him about what she was feeling, not yet anyway.

A couple of hours later, Parker walked Jayde up to the outside door of the apartment. He wanted to come inside, but there was still this lingering worry about whether or not Joe would be ticked off that he came up the stairs with her.

Jayde could see the hesitation in Parker's eyes, and told him, "I think it will be okay. We'll be like ninjas." She smiled.

Laughing, Parker followed her.

They were standing on the landing next to Jayde's front door when they heard Joe's door open.

Turning, Jayde pinned Parker up against the wall away from the railing. She wasn't even sure why she did it, but having him so close was extremely nice.

They listened to Joe's footsteps as he went downstairs. The front door opened and they heard Joe yell, "Have a good day," before the door shut.

Jayde broke first, laughing into Parker's jacket.

As Parker listened to Jayde's laugh, he felt like for the first time he understood what true contentment was. This was what he saw with his parents for years but never could pinpoint how they achieved it.

"Jayde," He whispered.

She looked up at Parker and smiled, the laughter still lingering on her features. "Yes," She said.

Parker searched her eyes. "How is this happening so fast?" He asked out loud.

Jayde knew what he was asking, but she had no idea how to answer him. "I don't know," She responded honestly. Her voice was only a whisper because her heart beating so hard wasn't letting her catch her breath.

Leaning down, Parker slowly moved to kiss Jayde. He liked to watch her eyes when they anticipated his kisses. They widened and he could see specks of gold mixed in with the blue.

As their lips met for the kiss, Jayde thought she might actually melt. Logically, it wasn't possible but, in her mind, Parker's kisses were so hot that it was a real thing. "Hmmm," She purred as his lips covered hers more fully.

They stood there, wrapped up in one another, kissing. There was no rush, no crazy, just the pure pleasure of being together and learning about one another.

Parker loved Jayde's lips, but he wanted to kiss her elsewhere too. Pulling away just enough to break the connection between their lips, he turned his head slightly and began placing soft kisses on the side of Jayde's neck.

Not sure when she became so sensitive on her neck, Jayde felt her body responding in ways she didn't know it would. Her belly was tight and everything throbbed, but in a completely wonderful way.

"Uh, Parker," Jayde whispered, trying to find a small part of her brain to work correctly.

He only stopped long enough to make a noise that sounded like, "Hmm," and then kept on kissing Jayde's neck.

With a sigh, Jayde was able to pull away far enough to look up into Parker's eyes. They were dark with desire, she imagined her own looked the same way to him. "I was just thinking, maybe we should go inside."

Jayde's suggestion turned Parker's stomach upside down. He didn't imagine there was anything else he wanted more at the moment than going into Jayde's apartment. If he did, though, he knew they'd sleep together. "I want to, so badly, but I can't," He whispered.

It wasn't difficult to see that Parker was torn. It made him more attractive to Jayde. She was feeling pretty crazy at the moment herself. "I understand, but I don't have to like it."

Parker half laughed, "Oh, you are something aren't you?"

Tilting her head, Jayde baited him, "What do you mean, something?"

Now Parker was being drawn into sexual awareness, but a whole new kind. "Oh, you look at me with those pretty eyes, and act all innocent, but you and I both know if I come inside, I'm not leaving for a while and we'll end up making love." His eyes grew serious, and then he added, "And, I do want you Jayde, more than anything."

"I want you too, Parker," Jayde admitted, her voice only a whisper because she was so keyed up.

Leaning back against the wall, Jayde still in his arms, Parker asked her, "So what do you propose we do about this?"

Playing with Parker's collar, and lightly touching his neck with her fingertips, Jayde gave him a long look. "I guess I'll send you home, Parker, but this will be the last time I do." She swallowed hard because she could see Parker's response to her words, and that caused her own strong response. "The next time we are at this point, I want you, all of you, to myself." She felt strong because she could get him to respond this way. "And I'll need lots of time to make sure I do it right."

Parker wasn't sure if he would be able to say goodbye to Jayde. Her words drove him nuts. He cursed himself as he held her close and kissed her. This kiss was something he did to possess her and let her know, without words, that he understood.

Consumed, that was the only word Parker could come up with to describe the kiss they were sharing now. His lips tried to dominate Jayde's but she met him, kiss for kiss, and didn't let him have the control he wanted. He knew that this was escalating quickly and he needed to leave or he wouldn't.

Jayde pouted when he pulled away. Even knowing it was childish, she couldn't help it. Kissing Parker was far more preferable to anything else she could think of at the moment. "I get lonely when you stop kissing me," She murmured.

Hearing those words from Jayde made Parker's insides go nuts. "And every time you say something like that to me, I don't want to leave you."

Giving Parker a squeeze, she replied, "I know we just said we wouldn't take this further today, but I can't help telling you the truth."

"And I never realized how much hearing the truth would make me go crazy," Parker responded.

Jayde leaned up and gave him one more kiss. "And now, I need to send you home. I'll call you in a few days and we'll make a date that may include an overnight clause, if you're open to it."

Parker actually growled, and leaned in to give Jayde a quick kiss before, very reluctantly, letting her go.

It was like having cold water thrown on her, so Jayde took a step back. She didn't anticipate this much reluctance in letting Parker leave. "I think I'll make that our goodbye otherwise you'll never get out of here."

Parker stepped back, away from Jayde, and already missed her. "I'll be waiting for your call," He told her, and started down the stairs.

Jayde stood there, leaning over the railing, and watched Parker make his way downstairs. When he reached the bottom floor, he looked up at her, and smiled. Jayde smiled back, but couldn't say anything. Even after she heard the front door close, she stood on the landing, just looking down.

Parker made it home, shut the front door, and heard his cell phone ring. "Hi mom," He said in greeting. "Before you say anything, I have to ask you some questions."

Chapter 10

Her alarm went off, and Jayde had to take a moment to wake up fully. She went to bed on time the night before, but tossed and turned most of the night, with thinking of Parker and how she never should have let him go home.

She got up and tried to go about her routine of stretching and showering. It was tough this morning, her thoughts drifting to Parker and wondering about how things would be between them when they did make love. It wasn't something Jayde spent a whole lot of time on normally. If she was in a relationship and wanted it to be physical, she discussed it. Being very cautious was part of being responsible so her actions were examined. Just thinking about Parker made her mind go crazy and obsessed with being with him. What was wrong with her?

Halfway through the morning, Sister Marjorie came into the shop. She smiled and waved at Jayde, and then found a seat near the window. Pulling out her bible, she read a passage, and then tucked it away when Jayde came over.

It took about ten seconds for Sister Marjorie to realize that Jayde was agonizing over something. She gave her order and waited.

Jayde brought Sister Marjorie's tea over to her, along with a muffin Joe baked within the last hour. She put down the order, smiled at the Sister, and was about to turn back toward the counter when Sister Marjorie asked, "Why don't you sit down and tell me what's on your mind?"

Standing there, Jayde wondered if this was a good idea. How did you talk to a nun about sex? Well, she decided she needed someone's advice on the subject. "Okay," She answered, and sat down across from the Sister.

"Now," Sister Marjorie told her young friend, "Tell me what's clearly eating at you."

Jayde looked around to make sure none of the other customers needed her. When she was reasonably sure no one would interrupt her, she turned back to face Sister Marjorie, and explained, "When I'm with Parker, I want everything, and I feel everything." She looked down at her clasped fingers, hoping they would give her the right words. "Yesterday, I wanted him to stay, and then we both decided it was too fast, but my body doesn't feel like it's too fast."

Sister Marjorie considered Jayde's words for a minute. "I remember that feeling," She answered back, and then wanted to laugh at the shocked look on Jayde's face. "I wasn't a nun from the day I was born," She smiled and reached over to squeeze Jayde's hands. "There was a young man, during my last summer at home, and we fell in love."

Jayde quickly looked around because she surely didn't want to be interrupted during this story. "Go on," She urged the Sister.

"Well," Sister Marjorie leaned in closely, "His name was Will and he was just so," she looked away dreamily remembering, "wonderful."

Getting anxious, Jayde asked, "What happened?"

Sister Marjorie's eyes came back to the present and a sad smile settled on her lips. "I was going to begin my training as a nun and he was going to start his training to be a priest."

If Jayde wasn't shocked before, she was now. "No," She whispered.

Smiling, Sister Marjorie, nodded. "Now he is a Bishop in Boston, and I'm here." She squeezed Jayde's hands once more. "We keep in touch here and there, and we're both sincerely fulfilled with our choices, but I get the impression we both suffer from a case of "what if," every now and again." Shrugging, the Sister added, "At least I have them, I can't specifically speak for Will."

Jayde sat back and sighed. First the revelation about her mother's talk and now this lost love talk from Sister Marjorie, it was all a little surreal. "I'm sad for you, but happy too, does that make sense?"

Sister Marjorie smiled, "It makes perfect sense." She took a sip of her tea, and replied, "Life is a series of choices, and sometimes the choice we make is the right one at first, sometimes we don't see the consequences of that choice for a time."

"Let's face it," Jayde said as she leaned back again, "I'm in love with him." Saying it made it real and Jayde had to fight the feeling of hyperventilating. "I don't know why, or how, or what the heck is going on, only that I want him, I want to be with him, and it's driving me nuts."

Being still, Sister Marjorie took in Jayde's words. "I guess," She finally said, "that you have to decide what to do about this."

Jayde rolled her eyes, "Not exactly the advice I was hoping for here."

"I'm sure it isn't," Sister Marjorie replied, "but it's your life, only you can choose."

One of her customers called her over so Jayde excused herself from the table and went over to help them. It was a welcomed break from the conversation with Sister Marjorie. Who, as it turned out, wasn't at all who Jayde thought she was. By the time she finished with the customers, Sister Marjorie was gone. She left a note, along with some money for her order, on the table. Jayde picked up the note and read it....

Call me if you need me. Do what your heart tells you, pray about it.

For some reason, reading the note did help Jayde.

Parker sat in his office for most of the day. He met with a few clients, answered dozens of emails, and gave a new client a quote for his services. Yet, he wasn't even sure if he did anything right. His mind was preoccupied with a certain beautiful barista.

Owen stood in the door to his boss' office, and waited. Something was going on and he couldn't take the suspense any longer. When Parker finished up his email, and turned around, Owen spoke up. "Are you going to tell me what's going on with you?"

Parker was lost in his thoughts and didn't see Owen standing there until he spoke. "Uh, I don't understand what you mean," He replied, hoping that his assistant would drop it.

Crossing the space between the doorway, and his boss's desk, Owen plopped down in a chair that faced Parker. "Well, you've been sort of walking around like you've been drugged or something."

Becoming irritated, Parker calmly put his hands down on his desk, and replied with, "I've not been drugged, and nothing is going on with me," he tried to use his most business-like tone.

Not believing a word his boss said, Owen crossed his arms. It was time to bring out the big guns. "Well, what would you say if I told you that a Miss Jayde Greene called and wanted you to call her back?" As soon as the words left his lips, he saw the change in Parker's whole demeanor.

"She did?" Parker asked, looking for his cell phone.

Owen cleared his throat, "No, actually, but I wanted to see your face when I mentioned the young lady's name."

Not amused, Parker scowled at his assistant.

Standing back up, Owen started toward the door. "In the time that I've worked for you, I have never seen you so distracted." As he passed through the doorway, he threw out, "And it's pretty entertaining."

Parker watched Owen leave and was really upset. Although he had no earthly idea why. After leaving Jayde yesterday, he thought he had it figured out, and then after talking to his mom, everything was all confusing. No matter which way he looked, there was chaos. For someone like him, who dealt with avoiding chaos, it was very unnerving. And then when he thought he had it figured out, he'd have this image of Jayde after she kissed him pop into his mind and his insides went to mush.

Jayde was cleaning up the shop, and Joe was in the back, when there was a knock on the shop door. It was Connor. Smiling, Jayde went over and opened the door. "What's up, Connor?" She asked.

Flushed, Connor came inside the shop. "Jayde," He gushed, "the girl I asked to prom said yes."

Giving him a quick hug, Jayde smiled. "Was she surprised?"

Nodding eagerly, Connor answered, "Oh yeah, it was epic."

"Epic?" Jayde asked. "Wow, you're a lucky guy."

Connor blushed, "Yeah, I am."

After Connor left, Jayde finished cleaning up with a huge smile on her face. It was a nice distraction from the thoughts that seemed to spin around in her mind regarding Parker. Seeing the happiness on Connor's face was just the pick-me-up she needed.

She was finishing up when Joe came out of the back. He looked around and told Jayde, "Looks good, let's go."

Shaking her head at his lack of conversation, Jayde nodded, and told him, "I'm ready."

Twenty minutes later, she was up in her apartment, looking through a magazine while her dinner heated in the microwave, when her phone rang. Seeing it was Parker, Jayde answered with, "I thought I was supposed to call you."

"Are you kidding me?" Parker asked her. "After those kisses yesterday, could I think of anything else?"

Blushing, and glad that Parker couldn't see her blushing, Jayde mumbled, "Really?"

"Yes, really," Parker replied, "and even my assistant was teasing me about it."

Jayde's interest intensified. She smiled, then asked, "And what was he saying?"

Sighing, Parker leaned against the counter in his kitchen. He was supposed to making something to eat, but couldn't get his mind right until he talked to Jayde. "He was saying that I was distracted and said that you called," He rushed to say, "and then he admitted that you didn't call but he wanted to see if my reaction meant that you were the reason for my distraction."

"And what did you tell him?" Jayde asked, baiting him.

Turning to walk through the living room, Parker answered, "Well, I didn't really say anything. I don't want to tell him anything, I just want to talk to you."

His words were making the want in Jayde multiply in it's intensity. "I see you've decided to lay it all out there." She said, and was happy that he did.

"Well," Parker said into the phone, "if you can, so can I."

It was easy to get lost in his words and in the feelings that Parker brought out in her. Jayde welcomed the draw of it all. She also knew that the speed in which they were going was fast and she would be lying if all the revelations about her parents and Sister Marjorie weren't making her pause a little. "I want you, but I'm worried."

Parker's whole demeanor changed with one sentence. "What is it?" He asked, concerned, and wishing he could hold her.

"I've had some pretty interesting conversations with people lately and I just don't want to make a mistake," She said, picking up a kitchen towel and twisting it around her hands.

Parker listened to what she was saying, but had to ask, "So you think we'd be making a mistake?"

Panic filled Jayde's chest, "No," she said first, and then said, "I don't know." There was silence on the other end, so she tried to explain, "It's just this thing between us is growing into its own thing and I'm feeling a little like I've been thrown in the deep end here."

Although Parker understood what she was saying, since he'd basically had that same mental battle going on in his head, her words still stung. "I understand," He told her, but even he heard the disappointment in his own voice.

"Parker," Jayde said, trying to get them back to where they were before, "Please don't."

He knew she was trying to ease things over but Parker didn't want that. For the first time in his life, he wasn't playing it safe. He wanted her, wanted what was between them, and he wasn't going to be quiet about it. She wasn't that much younger than he was so he knew she knew what was going on. "Don't what?" He asked, "Don't pour out my heart and hope you take it?"

Jayde's heart was aching, "It's not like that, I'm just having some jitters, I think I'm allowed."

There was an edge to her voice, Parker heard it, and he knew she heard it. "I'll tell you what," He began, "You call me when you're ready to follow through on what you've been telling me for the last week. How much you want to be with me, how tough it is to leave me," the hurt was permeating the words, "and when you're one hundred percent sure, which I might add, you'll never be, you just call me up."

Tears started escaping down Jayde's cheeks. He was right, she was being a coward and said the wrong thing. "Parker," She whispered.

He didn't want to hear any excuses, "Goodnight, Jayde."

Jayde stood in her kitchen and looked down at her cell phone, saying call ended.

The next morning, Joe met Jayde at the landing outside of his apartment. With one look at her, and he knew what happened. If there was one thing that he'd picked up on over the years, it's the look of a crushed woman. "What the hell did he do?" He demanded.

Hearing the anger in Joe's voice actually made Jayde chuckle. "It wasn't him, Joe, it was me," Jayde explained. "It was a stupid misunderstanding."

Even though Joe gave her a curt nod, he already planned on having a talk with that young man.

It was crazy to Jayde's way of thinking. Just the day before she was keyed up thinking that her relationship with Parker was going to go further, and with one stupid conversation, the whole thing just blew up in her face.

Later in the morning, when she was in between customers, Jayde just kept thinking about the phone call over and over again. She didn't reject him, although that's what he thought, she only said she was scared. Who the hell wouldn't be scared? She asked herself. You just meet someone, and you just have this instant chemistry, and you just

want to spend every single day with them, and then you want to sleep
with them, and then your mind starts thinking about the future...... It
was insane! How could he not understand that she just wanted to take
a minute to think it through?

Joe stood in the kitchen, looking over the counter that separated
him from the front counter. She was thinking again, just like she had
been all day. For some reason, another face came to his mind and Joe
stopped himself.

Chapter 11

The week was ending, and Jayde was relieved. It was far more work to get through the day pretending to be okay, than it was to actually be okay. Her thoughts were constantly on Parker; wondering what he was doing, was he thinking about her, was he fixating on it all the way she was?

She was surprised when Joe told her, "Just take off, Connor and I have this."

Normally, Jayde would have just stayed but she was so sad, that it was a relief to go up to her apartment.

She trudged up the stairs, each step seeming interminable. Instead of two flights, it seemed more like twenty.

Even Mr. Beethoven knew something was up. All week he'd been very affectionate and that wasn't his style, being a cat and all. As he had every other night, he wound his way around Jayde's legs and purred almost the minute she walked through the door.

The tears started falling then, and Jayde was angry because she couldn't stop them. Not that tears were bad, just that she didn't want to cry because of something so ridiculous.

Her mother always told her that, "To hold onto pride and not communicate is its own form of rejection." She didn't understand that phrase until now. She knew it would be easy to just call Parker and ask him to forgive her. They might even be able to salvage a night this weekend. But, the fear she told him about stopped her. Oh, she wanted him, more than anything, but the fear held her back. Fear of what, she wasn't sure, but it was there and she couldn't shake it.

After getting ready for bed, Jayde flipped the television on and was channel-surfing when she settled on the weather report. The weatherwoman was saying, "And several hurricanes are in the Atlantic. We believe they might become a problem for the Gulf Coast within the next week. We'll keep you posted."

Hearing that news did nothing to improve Jayde's mood. She'd gone through Hurricane Ike and it was a very scary experience. Luckily, she was Felicia and her family, but they still had to contend with pretty significant damage. Jayde made a mental note to talk to Joe about it the next day.

Parker stood in his kitchen and couldn't remember what he came into the room for. Was he hungry? Was he getting a pen? Who the hell knew. For the last couple of days, he was miserable, walking around doing the bare minimum amount of thinking to get through the day. Owen went from teasing him about Jayde to avoiding him almost completely. On the few occasions his assistant was brave enough to engage in conversation, Parker managed to snap at him. It wasn't like Parker to act this way, he was just upset.

And Jayde, he thought to himself, what was Jayde doing? Was she as miserable as he was? Even only knowing her for the short time he had, he imagined that she was as tormented as he was.

After he hung up with her Monday, he knew that he wasn't right. Neither was she, but he shouldn't have been so harsh with her. If someone had told him he'd meet her and fall so hard, so fast, he would've laughed. And yet, here it was, his heart was lost and he had no idea how to get her to talk to him.

He was still standing in the kitchen when his phone rang. "Hello," He answered absently.

Silvia knew immediately that not all was well with her son, "Parker, do you want to talk about it?" She asked, dismissing the reason she called him in the first place.

"Hey, mom," Parker responded, then sighed. "Uh, no, just a misunderstanding."

Unsure about asking the question, Silvia decided to risk it. "Is it about this young lady you're dating? Jayde is her name, right?"

Although Parker knew he'd told his mom about Jayde when they spoke the previous Sunday, he was still surprised that she pegged that as the problem so quickly. "Uh, yeah, but I really don't want to talk about this with you, mom, I hope you're not offended."

With a huff, Silvia answered, "Of course I'm offended. Any mother believes that her children will tell her everything about everyone forever. Even if it's crazy, as mothers, we all still hope."

Her words made Parker smile, and he was pretty sure they were intended to do just that. "I'm working on the problem, mom, but I promise to call you if I can't work it out in a reasonable amount of time."

Knowing her opinion had just been dismissed, Silvia hedged her bets, and told him, "Well, time is relative and very different between men and women. You'd be wise to remember that."

"I will, mom, what did you call about?" He remembered that she called him.

He spoke to his mom about a couple of fundraisers that she and Parker's father were heading in the next couple of months. Parker and his brother, Reece, were expected to attend and contribute. It was the least they could do to show respect to their parents. Until now, Parker never minded. But, if he didn't get this situation with Jayde resolved, he feared he would be useless for anything else.

On Sunday, Jayde went to church. She felt very disconnected and needed some support, even if it was just by being around other people. She'd been keeping to herself, just going out to go to work, and then coming home. She thought even Mr. Beethoven was getting sick of her sulking. When you think your cat is mad, it's time to take action.

She was sitting in church, listening to the sermon. It was about forgiveness. Forgiving others but also forgiving yourself. The message hit Jayde right in the heart.

Sister Marjorie came over and sat down after the service ended. She didn't even bother to ask Jayde how she was doing. The pain was written all over the young woman's face. "If you want to talk, I'm here," Was all she said.

Jayde sat there for a few more minutes, just thinking, and then she asked, "Why didn't you ask Will if he regretted both of your decisions to stay with the church?"

The Sister tried to find the right words, before answering, "Because his regrets or lack of them wouldn't have changed mine. I made that decision and, if I hadn't, would I have met you? Would I have met all the young people I've been Blessed to help over the years? Maybe I would have had a perfectly happy life married to Will and having children, but at the time, I made the decision I though was best for me."

"We had a fight," Jayde admitted. "I was telling him how afraid I was to allow our relationship to become physical and he thought I was rejecting him." She looked at Sister Marjorie, and swiped away a stray tear, before adding, "And he was right."

Patting Jayde's hand, Sister Marjorie said, "I'm not sure he was right, Jayde I've known you since you were, what? Eleven? And I've never heard you reject anyone. So, you had a moment's hesitation, maybe if more of us had those, then we wouldn't make some hasty decisions that have lasting consequences." She squeezed Jayde's hand again, "And did you having these fears really convince you not to take your relationship further, or did it force you to reevaluate whether it was the right decision in the first place?"

"You are very good at your job, you know that," Jayde said in a deadpan voice. She smiled when Sister Marjorie chuckled in response. "I want him, Sister, more than anything. It's not just his body, although that seems to be a subject I'm rather fixated on, it's just how he makes me feel, how I think I make him feel."

Sister Marjorie considered Jayde's words, before replying, "It sounds a lot like love to me, Jayde."

Smiling, Jayde told her, "It sounds like that to me too."

Jayde walked down the seawall after church. She felt lighter emotionally. Her decisions were made and she decided not to let the fear keep her from Parker. Now, if she could only be sure he would feel the same.

Parker was finishing up a meeting with a client on Monday morning, when Owen slipped a pile of phone messages onto his desk. He'd somewhat mended his attitude at work, in light of realizing he was behaving like a child. Owen seemed to understand and they'd moved on.

As Parker was sifting through the messages, he stopped when he read the one from Joe Trenton. Standing up, he walked out to Owen's office, and asked, "This Joe Trenton, did he say if he worked in Galveston?"

Owen looked up briefly since he was trying to compose some cover letters for new clients. "He said you'd know who he was," He said absently.

The pit in his stomach was growing wider as Parker walked back into his own office. He'd never been a coward, and he wouldn't start now. Slowly, he dialed the number on the message, and waited.

"Bout time you called," Joe said in a gruff voice.

Parker cleared his throat, and responded, "Yes sir, sorry, I was in a meeting."

Joe nodded, "So, let's talk about what you did to hurt Jayde and what you're going to do to make it better."

Although Parker was glad that Joe got to the point of the call, it was still unsettling how Joe's voice over the phone could intimidate. "Sir," He started, "With all due respect, I think that Jayde and I will have to work this out between ourselves."

"I've no doubt about it, son, but listen, she's miserable and I'm going to give you some information that will help, if you've got a brain in that head of yours," Joe said gruffly.

Listening, Parker began to smile.

Jayde met up with Felicia the next day, hoping a friendly face would help her get out of her emotional rut. Even with resolving a few things about her feelings regarding Parker, she couldn't bring herself to call him. She blurted out the story to Felicia over lunch at a nearby diner. Joe was rather happy to have her take off for an extended break, and that unnerved her too.

Felicia listened quietly until Jayde was finished, and then sat there, a look of shock on her face. When she did speak, she started with, "Wow. Just wow."

"I know," Jayde replied.

Placing her head in her hand. Felicia thought for a few seconds before saying, "If I could find one guy who made me feel what you're describing, and doing what Parker has done for you, I think I would've married him after only a week."

Sighing, Jayde smiled weakly.

"I'm not saying you did anything wrong," Felicia rushed. "I can see it, what you describe, in your face when you say his name." She took a quick sip of her iced tea. "What I'm having trouble getting is that you seem to have figured out what you want, but you still haven't called him?"

The question Felicia asked was the same one that Jayde kept asking herself. "I'm being prideful, I know."

Leaning forward, Felicia asked her, "Would you rather go home to your cat and a microwave dinner, or would you like to be in Parker's arms?"

A slow smile spreading across her mouth, Jayde answered, "Point taken."

After Jayde got home, she was just picking up her laundry to take downstairs when there was a knock on her door.

Walking over, she opened it and there was Joe. "Hey, Joe, I was just about to do some laundry."

"Hurricane Harvey is on his way and he may take a swipe at us," Joe explained. "I'm going to be doing putting up some plywood over the windows tomorrow so I need you to make sure you've got the area cleared."

Since Jayde had only two windows, she didn't think it would be that difficult. "Sure, Joe," She told him, and then asked, "That's the reason you came up here?"

Joe was uncomfortable saying what he had to say, but he took a deep breath, and said, "That young man of yours is downstairs and I don't want him up here if it's gonna upset you."

Her heartrate speeding up, Jayde reached up and kissed Joe's cheek. "You're a sweetheart, it's fine."

Parker was standing inside the entryway leading up to Jayde's apartment. He made the arrangements but still wasn't sure that Jayde would go along with it. He'd run into Joe as he came up to the door and explained why he was here. Joe told him to, "stay put, so I can check with Jayde."

Now Joe was coming back downstairs and his facial expression didn't give anything away. Parker's palms were sweating, and he waited.

Joe wanted to let the boy sweat it for a minute more, even though he thought it was kinda mean. Finally, he told Parker, "She'll be right down."

With a respectful nod, Parker allowed Joe to go by him to leave. Within a minute, he heard the door to Jayde's apartment close and he could hear her steps as she came downstairs. The noise seemed to echo off the walls, making Parker even more nervous.

When she stepped down onto the first floor, Jayde thought her heart was going to beat right out, and hop out along the sidewalk. She was sure that Parker could hear it too. "Hi," She said shyly.

Parker stepped toward her, "Hi," he replied. "I know you may still be mad, but I wanted to say that I was an ass and I shouldn't have said what I said to you."

Relief poured through Jayde's chest. "Oh Parker," She almost whined. Closing the few feet between them, she ran into his arms. "I'm sorry too, it was stupid."

Putting her away from him, so he could look into her eyes, Parker said, "No, it wasn't stupid. You are scared, so am I, and frankly our argument didn't make any sense."

Jayde nodded, allowing happy tears to fall down her cheeks.

"Oh, my beautiful lady," Parker whispered as he wiped the tears from her cheeks, "I don't ever want to make you cry."

Shaking her head in denial, she told him, "I'm making myself cry." She hugged him close. "We'll just have to work on it."

"Sounds like a plan," Parker whispered into her hair as he held her to him. "But I have a little surprise for you."

Jayde smiled against his chest, "Really?" She asked.

Parker smiled. This was how it was supposed to be, him making her happy. "Yep, a little adventure, if you're up to it."

Jayde stepped back. "Do I look like a girl who's afraid of a little adventure?" She asked, her eyes flickering with mischievous glee.

"Nope," Parker said, "thank goodness."

They walked out of the building together.

Parker helped her get into his car, a smile plastered on his face.

Jayde wondered what they were doing. It was the curiosity she held onto every day, but didn't want to irritate Parker with asking about it.

They drove up the freeway toward Houston.

Jayde started to wonder then because she knew she shouldn't stay out too late tonight with having to be at work at four a.m. the next morning. Although, the adventurous part of her said to 'stop whining and go with it.'

After an hour, Jayde did cave in and ask, "Where are we going?"

Parker smiled, and answered, "Almost there."

Another twenty minutes passed and they pulled into the Galleria. It was a very upscale shopping mall in Houston. Jayde had only been there a handful of times because the trek up was long, and because she didn't see any need to purchase things from the high-end stores located in the mall. She shot Parker a confused look, but didn't say anything.

They parked and got out, Parker guiding her.

It was a weeknight so there weren't as many people here as the last time Jayde came with Felicia on a weekend.

They walked inside and started to go down the main corridor of the mall.

"Are we shopping?" Jayde asked Parker.

He gave her a sideways look, and said, "Not exactly."

A few minutes later, he came up to a half wall and leaned against it. Jayde joined him and looked in front of them. It was a huge indoor ice skating rink.

"I could've given you flowers or candy, but I thought you might appreciate this more." Parker moved behind her and wrapped his arms around her waist.

Pure joy filled Jayde's heart. "Oh yes," She giggled.

Chapter 12

Parker held her hand as they got the ice skates at the counter. He helped her lace hers up and then did his own. They both laughed as Jayde tried to get up on her blades to walk the mere eight feet or so to the edge of the ice rink.

Even though Jayde thought she was a graceful person, there was no gracefulness to be found. She wobbled on the blades, acting like a baby who was taking their first steps. Watching Parker walk confidently beside her, she was jealous of his actual grace.

Gently stepping out onto the ice, Jayde's hands were gripping the rail around the edge of the rink like it was her only link to surviving. Parker was on the outside, there if she needed to lean on him.

A few minutes later, and only feeling slightly more confident, Jayde told him, "Why don't you skate for a few minutes and I'll get over my fear."

Chuckling, Parker shook his head no. "I'll just stay with you."

Shooing him with her hands, Jayde insisted, "No, I want to watch you skate and know what I'm trying to strive for."

Still unsure, Parker was reluctant.

"Go!" Jayde told him in a louder voice.

He turned then and skated off.

Jayde managed to get herself turned around, and somewhat stable, so she could watch Parker. He glided around the rink, zigging and zagging around other skaters. She couldn't get over how smooth his movements were. It was kind of mesmerizing, just watching Parker's keen skill. When he came back to her, sliding in on the edge of the blades, she was surprised, and laughed. "Wow that was amazing."

Parker blushed a little. "Not so much, I'm pretty rusty." He moved around so he was holding onto Jayde's arm. He helped her turn so she could move around the edge of the rink. "But, you are looking at a 2002 Divisional Champion." He lifted up his fist and hollered, "Go Bulldogs!"

Jayde hadn't really seen this kid-like side of Parker, and it was adorable. "Go Bulldogs," She copied his enthusiasm, and they both laughed.

After about twenty minutes, Jayde allowed Parker to help her get away from the edge of the rink, and move out onto the open ice. It was scary, but exciting too.

She was thinking that the other skaters would plow into them, but everyone seemed to just smoothly glide around everyone else. Jayde was thankful that there were a few more newcomers like herself. Parker was immensely patient and helped her whenever she needed it.

When it was time to go, she was almost sad to take off her skates. Although there was the reassurance that she could actually walk on her own now. It was still very nice to lean against Parker, however better because she wasn't afraid she'd take him down with her. "Oh, Parker," She sighed as they walked out of the mall and towards his car, "That was so much fun."

Parker smiled. Again, he couldn't get over how happy Jayde was to do something that was relatively simple. He'd forgotten how much he liked to skate. She made him see things he'd simply overlooked before now. "I'm glad you liked it, I know your first time can be unnerving."

Blushing, Jayde wondered if he was just talking about ice skating, or other things too. "Yes, it can," She agreed.

The increase in temperature around them gave Parker a moment's pause. One second they were like kids, and the next, well, they were definitely not kids. He decided to let the comment drop, and helped her into the car.

They spent the drive back to Galveston talking about childhood adventures. Jayde spoke of the museums and art galleries her mother took her to, while Parker talked about his brother, Reece, and how much trouble they got into while playing with their neighborhood friends.

Parker just finished a particularly funny story about covering the neighbor's dog with kool-aid powder so he looked like a rainbow.

Jayde was laughing, and asked him, "Can you tell me about your parents?"

After taking a deep breath, Parker said, "Sure," he thought for a few seconds and then began. "My mom, Silvia, is a magazine editor who does so many things at one time that I'm pretty sure her head would fall off if she tried to fit anymore in." He winked at Jayde and turned back to the road. "My dad, Glenn, is a doctor, and the most laid-back doctor I've ever met. He is driven but you'd never know it."

Listening to Parker talk about his parents, made Jayde happy and sad. She was happy that Parker's voice was full of caring when he talked about them, but sad because it made her miss her mother. "And how did they meet?" She asked, trying to distract herself from those thoughts.

"Well," Parker smiled, "My dad was a sophomore in college and he'd just passed a big Chemistry final." He stopped only long enough to change lanes on the freeway, and shoot Jayde a quick smile. "He was coming out of the building on campus and wasn't paying attention. He literally ran into my mom, and basically sent all of her books and papers flying. She called him some pretty awful names, and he told Reece and I that he knew from that moment, that she was the woman for him."

Jayde giggled, "No," she commented.

"I swear, that's what he told us," Parker made a cross over his heart with his hand.

Parker, feeling like they'd gotten so close, asked her, "How did your parents meet?" It wasn't until the words were out of his mouth, that he realized what an insensitive question that was. Jayde already told him that she was raised by only her mother. "I'm sorry, Jayde, I didn't mean to ask something like that," He started to say.

Putting up her hands, Jayde told him, "It's okay, Parker, you were only trying to get to know me." She took a deep breath, and explained, "From what my mom told me, my father was part of a big company and he and his co-workers were all going through a big conference in California when they met. She said it was love at first sight."

Listening to her, Parker smiled. She had to know that no matter what the circumstances ended up being, that her parents did love one another. Just like his.

"She said they spent every day together, as much as they could around my father's job. The group ended up going out of the country for work and they didn't get a chance to really say goodbye." Jayde sighed. "From what my mom said, they hadn't even exchanged addresses so he didn't know where she'd gone. By the time she found out about me, she had no idea how to reach him."

Parker's smile faded. "That's so sad," He looked over at Jayde. She wasn't crying, and he was glad.

"Please," Jayde almost pleaded, "don't feel sorry for me, Parker." She didn't like it when people pitied her. "My life might not have been traditional, but my mom loved me so much."

Nodding, Parker agreed, "I've known a lot of kids who had both their parents but they didn't grow up with as much love as you describe."

A sad smile settled on Jayde's lips. She hated dwelling on sadness, but sometimes, it just showed up. She placed her hand over Parker's, and quietly said, "I really do feel Blessed, Parker. I had a wonderful, yet eccentric," she smiled, "mom and she always said that if my dad had known about me, then he would've been with us."

Parker couldn't help the fact that he felt awful for her. If what she said was true then her father had missed out just as much as she had. A parent and child just shouldn't go through that.

"I see the wheels turning, Parker Kinley," Jayde gave him a skeptical look.

He looked over and Parker just couldn't help the feeling of love that overwhelmed him when he was with this woman. "I'm allowed to think," He tried to sound defensive, but failed.

Jayde sighed, "You are, but don't get any ideas about a wonderful family reunion." She squeezed his hand. "I've tried everything I can think of to find him, and it's been a failure."

It hurt Parker to see the look of defeat in Jayde's eyes. The look was fleeting, but he still saw it. There was a part of her that was missing, and he wanted to help her find it if he could. "Well, let me know if you think of something else and I can help."

"I have been thinking of something," Jayde ran her fingers over Parker's hand very slowly.

He couldn't mistake the tone Jayde used, nor did he want to. It was seductive. "What is that?" He asked, knowing full well he was playing with fire.

Jayde knew he was thinking the same thing she was. It was difficult not to think about that. "It's that too, but that wasn't what I was referring too, not yet anyway."

Parker frowned, "Go on," he said.

"Well, I just wanted to say that I was miserable when we weren't speaking, even though it was only for few days, it was a very long few days."

Nodding in agreement, Parker decided not to speak, instead he let her talk.

Pulling her hands onto her lap, Jayde clasped her hands together. "I was thinking that I have more fun with you, doing silly things, than I do with anyone else." Sighing, Jayde reached over again, and smiled when he wound his fingers around hers. "I want you in all the ways that matter, but I know that the physical thing is a bit of an obstacle right now."

They were coming into Galveston, so the freeway ended. There were parking lots lining the side of the road. Parker found one, and pulled in. "It's not an obstacle for us, it's the step that changes things, Jayde."

Jayde nodded, "Yes, and it's going to be wonderful, I just know it, but I just need a little more time."

"And I'll give you whatever you need." He cupped her chin, "I hope you know that."

With the two of them in such close proximity, Jayde couldn't resist the temptation. She leaned over and kissed him. Once her lips tasted his, she wanted more. She reached up and clasped his shoulders to allow herself to move closer to him.

Jayde had to tear her lips away from Parker's. "See," She whispered, "it's me, I just want you so much, but I just keep going back and forth with that last hurdle."

"I'd hate it if you truly thought sleeping with me was a hurdle, but I understand your meaning." Parker smiled and tilted his forehead against Jayde's. "I promise you, it will be good, Jayde. I'll do everything I can to bring you pleasure."

With words like that, Jayde thought, who could resist him. "The thing is, Parker," She used the words slowly, "that you already bring me pleasure, I'm not sure if I could handle any more."

Parker chuckled, "Oh, I think you can handle a lot more," he tapped his fingertip on the end of her nose, and then leaned back up so he could drive again. Unfortunately, his pants were very uncomfortable now.

They drove back towards the shop, the awareness filling up the inside of the car like a balloon. It was getting to the point where it might explode.

In an effort to calm herself, Jayde tried to change the subject. "Joe tells me that Hurricane Harvey is on the way. They aren't sure if he'll hit Galveston or not."

A worried frown crossed Parker's face. "I heard a little but haven't been keeping up." He glanced over at Jayde and suggested, "How about if it's coming toward Galveston, you come up and hide out at my place for a few days."

Her eyebrows raised, Jayde tossed around the thoughts in her mind. "You mean, you and me locked away in your house while a storm rages outside?" Her voice low and sultry as she asked.

"Well, once you put it that way, how about we start tonight?" He asked, only halfway joking with her.

Jayde wished she could just run away with him. Looking down at her phone, she saw the time and groaned inwardly. "I'll have to take a raincheck, excuse the pun." She sighed. "I have to be up at four a.m."

That time was just horrible in Parker's mind. "I know, and I'm only half serious about the offer."

Play slapping his arm, Jayde pretended to pout. She knew if there was a way around all of their daily routines, she'd have to find it. But, tonight wasn't the night. What they both wanted would require time. She didn't think that rushing anything would be good when it came to making love with Parker.

Watching Jayde think made Parker smile. His dad always murmured, "Uh oh," when his mother was thinking. He told his sons, "there is something a little ominous when a woman is thinking that hard about something." Parker remembered his dad laughing after that but seeing Jayde's expression now, he understood the words much better.

As he pulled up to the curb in front of the shop, Parker glanced up and saw the curtains in Joe's apartment being pulled closed. Joe would hold on to his word, and Parker admired that about him.

Jayde reluctantly got out of Parker's car. She all but trudged around the front of it, like a kid who didn't want to go to school. Once Parker gathered her up into his arms though, all was better. Feeling secure, Jayde squeezed him tight, and whispered, "Thank you."

"It's me who should be thanking you," Parker spoke over the top of her head as he held her to him. "I'd really forgotten how much fun skating could be."

Leaning back, Jayde looked up into his eyes, "I hate it when I forget something so simple."

Parker nodded, "Me too."

He walked her up to the door, kissed her once more, and then slowly walked back to his car.

Jayde stepped inside the entryway, and locked the door behind her. She stood by the door and watched Parker drive off. Every time they parted, it became more difficult to leave.

The next morning, Jayde was up quickly, a smile on her face. When she walked down to the shop with Joe, she had to stifle a laugh when he commented, "Bout time you smile again."

They were swamped! Customers were coming in and out quickly, everyone talking about Hurricane Harvey. Joe turned on the small television in the back of the kitchen so they could hear updated weather reports and predictions. Right now, the storm was headed southwest of Galveston and everyone hoped it stayed that way.

After Connor arrived for his shift, Joe went upstairs and started putting up the plywood over the windows. He had it specially cut, and labeled for each window on the building. When not in use, they were stored up in the attic. It was a real pain getting them down, but Joe said it was necessary. A lot of businesses were starting to prepare. Some were clearing out display windows, and others were pulling up all the products and getting them off the floor. Flooding was the most immediate concern. People always thought it was the wind, but here, it was flooding.

By the end of the day, everyone was keyed up and emotionally exhausted. All anyone could talk about was the hurricane.

When Jayde made it upstairs to her apartment, she fell onto the bed and took a few deep breaths to relax.

Chapter 13

Parker just arrived home and called Jayde. "Hey," He said when she picked up. "I am home and it's a madhouse out there."

"Here too," Jayde told him. "A lot of prep work for the businesses."

Nodding, Parker turned on his television and turned it to the weather channel. "Did you see the amount of rain they expect us to get?"

Jayde sighed. She'd had this conversation about twenty times just in the last hour she was at work. "Yes, I heard," She said, her voice dry.

Parker could hear the change in her tone. "I'm sorry," He wanted to be supportive, "I'm sure there on the island is worse."

"Um hmm," Jayde said absently. She managed to stand up and walk into the kitchen to make some tea.

He could hear Jayde doing something, and felt like he was annoying her, "Should I call later?"

Realizing she was being rude, Jayde told him, "I'm sorry, I'm just tired and have been having the same conversation all day." She poured the water into her cup and absently stirred it. "I am just beat. I guess I'm worried too."

Understandable, Parker thought. "Is this your first hurricane?"

Jayde smiled, "No, I was here during Ike."

"A rough one," Parker commented.

Blowing on the mug, Jayde tried to calm her stress. "It was pretty bad but we were safe. I was with Felicia and her family."

Parker was relieved that Jayde wasn't alone, then or now.

He was away on vacation with friends when Ike hit, and his parents' house didn't sustain any real damage so it never occurred to Parker to worry about it. Listening to Jayde, he realized that not everyone was so unscathed by the hurricanes and their aftermath. "Do you want me to pick you up and you can stay here?"

Even though she was touched by Parker's offer, she couldn't leave Joe. She sighed before saying, "Parker, you're sweet to offer, but I want to be here for Joe and the coffee shop."

It was tough, feeling the sting of rejection. Even though, rationally, Parker knew she wasn't really rejecting him, she just had a strong connection to Joe's Cuppa Joe, and to Joe himself. "I understand," He told her, but there was a little part of him that didn't.

Hearing the sadness in Parker's words made Jayde take pause. "I'm sorry, Parker." She took a sip of her tea. "I do want to be there, with you, but I know that Joe is worried and that makes me worried."

Parker nodded, and replied, "I know, it's just being alone with you, for a few days, here, was something I'd been thinking about."

Jayde didn't even try to pretend she didn't know what he was talking about. "I think I'd wear you out, Mr. Kinley," She teased.

Her words were clear, and Parker's body jump to a level of arousal in moments. "Hmmm," He teased back, "I guess we'll just have to see about that."

Never backing down from a challenge, Jayde laughed. "I assure you that we will see about that."

He liked the way this conversation was going. "I'll have you know, Ms. Greene, that I really enjoy a challenge."

"I do too, Mr. Kinley," Jayde said.

When Jayde used that soft and slow tone, it drove Parker crazy. "I suppose I should hang up now, I've about reached the limit of my control."

Giggling, Jayde baited him just a bit more, "I see, well, I'll be sure to test the limits of your control the next time we see one another."

Clearing his throat, because talking was way too difficult in the physical state he was in, Parker calmed himself enough to say, "I'll talk to you tomorrow. Goodnight."

"Good night," Jayde whispered, and then disconnected the call. She stood there, against the counter, and thought about Parker for a while.

The next morning, Jayde turned on the television. She never did it in the morning before work, preferring to do yoga to wake up. With Hurricane Harvey bearing down on Texas though, it was more important to figure out what was going on with that.

All the local stations were focused on the storm and their predictions on where it would make landfall. It looked like Corpus Christi would be the area where Harvey said "hello" to Texas, and Jayde prayed for those who would be in the path of the hurricane. It was one of those weird situations where relief was present, but you knew that your relief was someone else's possible hurt. After Ike, Jayde knew that things could change in a few short hours. Rows of houses were either majorly damaged, or in some cases, completely gone or they were untouched.

It took all of Jayde's faith to keep her from being sucked into an abyss of sadness. She turned off the television and finished getting ready for work.

It was Thursday, and Parker decided to stay home for the rest of the week. He'd called Owen the night before and told him not to bother coming into the office. They'd already moved all of the files in the office into plastic bins and placed them up on the upper shelves to keep them from getting wet. All of Parker's files were backed up on an outside server so he wasn't worried about losing anything should the power be out or his office computers were damaged.

At home, he just sort of walked around. In the area that he lived, no one had ever had any flooding. That's what all the neighbors said anyway. Everyone seemed to be out on their front lawns, talking to everyone else about Harvey and his landfall.

Almost every few minutes, Parker's mind would drift to Jayde, and wonder what she was doing.

The shop was busier than usual for a weekday. There was usually a lull in foot traffic after the morning "rush" but today everyone seemed to be out. Most just looking for conversation about the storm. Jayde's nerves were frayed before the afternoon even hit.

Joe was his usual quiet self, except that he seemed to be spending a lot more time in the kitchen doing things. Even when Jayde expected him to take his mid-morning break, he stayed in the back.

Everyone seemed to clear out mid-afternoon so Joe made the decision to close early. Jayde was relieved. All of the drama of the situation was making her feel overwhelmed. She wanted the quiet of her apartment and Mr. Beethoven.

A few hours after she'd gotten home, Jayde felt caged in. Her apartment was usually her solace but now, it just felt too small. She knew it was because of the atmosphere. Everyone was feeling it. Joe was even quieter when he went home, as if that was even possible. He grumbled about "seeing her in the morning."

She picked up the phone and dialed Parker's number. When it went to voicemail, she felt even sadder. Deciding not to leave a message, Jayde hung up and went for a walk.

Parker went to the grocery store, just to stock up on the basics. Apparently, he wasn't the only person who had that idea. The store was jam-packed with people who were all trying to get the basics. One of his neighbors put in a generator a few years back, and offered to refrigerate anything if the power went out. Parker had spoken to his neighbors more in the last couple of days than he had in the last three years since he bought the house. It was nice to know that everyone was looking out for everyone else.

After he made it home, relatively intact, Parker put away his groceries, and sat down in a chair. Everyone was so keyed up that just getting through the store drained him. Not to mention, he was worried about Jayde, and Joe, and the shop. His phone rang and he answered without looking at the caller I.D. When his mother asked how he was holding up, Parker spilled out his thoughts.

"I'm okay, Mom, I'm just worried about Jayde." He admitted.

Silvia smiled knowingly. "How is she?" She asked her son.

Parker sighed. "I'm not sure actually." He answered.

It was difficult to watch your children struggle, and Silvia never wanted her boys to struggle with anything, much less a gift as wonderful as love. "She's being distant?" Silvia asked.

He didn't know how to answer at first. It was an overwhelming thing, feeling all of these things. "Yes, but she's worried about things down on the island, her boss, the coffee shop she works at."

Understanding, Silvia smiled. "But you wish that she'd be with you." It wasn't a question, but a statement.

"Yes," Parker paused, "No, I mean," he couldn't find the words so he stopped.

Silvia smiled. It was a lifetime ago that she felt all of those wonderful feelings for Glenn, and yet it seemed like yesterday. "Yes, you'd wish she was there with you, but no because you admire how much she cares for others and that's what made you fall in love with her in the first place."

Scary was the only word Parker could summon up in his mind. "You are a very scary woman sometimes Mom," He told her.

Now Silvia chuckled, "No, my sweet boy, it's just experience in falling in love. I was just thinking that it's been a long time since I had those feelings of indecision when I first fell in love with your father, but it sometimes seems like just yesterday."

"I was just thinking that it's only been two weeks and yet my life is empty without her." Parker admitted to his mom.

These were the moments that Silvia cherished. The ones when she felt like their sons needed her still. "I think that any woman who is as giving as Jayde is the only woman who could steal my son's heart."

They talked for a few minutes more, and Parker felt better after they hung up. It was nice to know that he wasn't the only one who ever got mixed up when falling in love. Looking down at his phone, he realized he'd missed a call from Jayde. He quickly hit the button to call her.

Jayde was in the middle of a yoga pose when her phone rang. She sat down and hit the connect button. "Hello there," She said softly. "I was just feeling boxed in and wanted to talk to you."

Hearing Jayde say those words was like a gentle breeze over his skin. It felt so soothing to him. "I was out fighting the masses at the grocery store," he explained.

"And how was that experience?" Jayde smiled.

Parker took a cleansing breath and answered, "Traumatic."

Laughing, Jayde gave Mr. Beethoven a quick scratch behind the ears as he passed by her. "We closed up early and I came home thinking I'd relax, but I just can't."

Nodding, Parker told her, "My mom called to make sure I was okay."

That was sweet, Jayde thought to herself, and then had a pang of envy because she wished her mother could call her. "I'm sure that was good."

"It was, she is a very knowledgeable woman," Parker responded, but didn't add anything.

Jayde wondered what meaning was behind his words, but decided that if he wanted her to know, he'd tell her.

Parker remarked, "And she asked how you were."

Surprised, Jayde replied with asking, "She did?"

"She did," Parker explained. "She knew I was missing you, Lord knows how, but it was a nice talk."

Laughing, Jayde told him, "Sometimes mothers are downright psychic."

Not wanting to make Jayde sad, talking about mothers, Parker changed the subject. "I know it's probably a waste of my breath but the offer to come up here still stands."

Smiling, Jayde's heartbeat sped up. "It's not a waste of your breath if it makes me realize how wonderful of a man you are, Parker."

Her words soothed his frazzled nerves.

"I would prefer to be up with you, but I'm needed here." Jayde tried to make him understand her responsibility.

Sighing, Parker told her, "I know, I'm just being selfish."

Now, Jayde was feeling a little bad for turning him down. "You are not selfish, Parker, I am very Blessed to have such an intelligent, handsome, and sexy man want me with him during a hurricane."

Although he knew she was teasing him, Parker still felt a thrill at the words.

"I'll tell you what," Jayde tried to soothe him, "As soon as Mr. Harvey has made his exit, let's plan something." She paused, trying to think of something, "Maybe a weekend up near Austin or something.

Smiling, she remembered a place her friend told her about a few months ago, "I heard about this great B&B from a friend, very romantic."

Parker was lost after Jayde said the word, "Weekend." He'd do whatever it took to make sure they had time together. "Promise?" He asked, sounding a little childish.

Jayde quickly caught onto his ploy. "Pinky swear," She said slowly, drawing out the words.

Laughing, Parker shook his head, and asked, "How on earth does anyone make the phrase, "pinky swear," sound so damn sexy?"

"I have no idea," Jayde replied while laughing, "But I'll try to do it more often if it makes you smile."

How could he not smile when Jaye was talking to him about future plans? How could he be so lost and yet feel so centered at the same time? The questions would have to be put off for a few more days. "Okay, I'll be a good boy and wait until we kick Harvey off the premises before I make any fun plans."

Jayde giggled, "That's a deal."

They hung up a few minutes later, and Jayde plopped down into the oversized chair in her living room. She was daydreaming about Parker when she heard a noise coming from the hallway outside her door. Figuring it was Joe, she decided to poke her head out.

As soon as Jayde opened the door, she saw the problem. Joe, in his independent nature, had been dropping down the large pieces of plywood down from the attic, by himself. In his determination, it appeared that one of the pieces wedged its way into the hole in the ceiling that led up to the attic.

Peeking around the large piece of plywood, Jayde called up, "Hey Joe, are you having a little trouble here."

He didn't answer but Jayde heard a string of expletives that made her laugh. It probably wasn't that funny to Joe, so she tried to tamp down on the noise. "Joe, how can I help?" She yelled up into the hole.

Twenty minutes, and two splinters later, Joe and Jayde managed to dislodge the plywood and get it down the stairs to the first floor.

There was a neat pile of it leaning against the wall, Jayde assumed it was for the windows of the shop. Joe told her earlier that those would be the last one covered so customers wouldn't wonder if the shop was open. It was a sweet thing and Joe scoffed at her when she told him that.

After she made sure Joe was done with the plywood, Jayde went back up to her apartment, and finished doing her yoga. For some reason, even with a hurricane bearing down, she felt very calm and happy. Parker Kinley was the reason.

Chapter 14

Friday was an omen from the beginning. When Jayde woke up, she could hear the wind picking up. Mr. Beethoven was hiding under the bed and no amount of coaxing from Jayde would bring him out. She was five minutes late getting out of the apartment which meant Joe gave her a look. And she didn't even get to do her yoga so she was half asleep as they went into the shop. Basically, she was frazzled.

Customers came pouring in right away, mostly local business owners who were in early to secure their own businesses. Joe had the television going and the volume up so everyone could hear the reports.

After the first hour, Jayde was already spent emotionally. She felt like she was holding onto her sanity by only a thin thread.

There was a slight lull, so she told Joe she was taking a five-minute break. He told her, "Make it fifteen."

As she walked upstairs, Jayde wondered what was getting to her so badly. She was safe, felt safe, and didn't doubt Joe when he told her everything would be okay. So why was she so crazed?

Opening up the door to her apartment, Jayde said, "Parker," out loud.

Parker woke up and stumbled out to the kitchen to make some coffee. Not having to go into work this morning, he decided to stay up late and catch up on some television shows he wanted to see. It was a distraction to keep his mind off of Jayde, and it didn't work very well. She occupied his mind almost non-stop and he thought maybe he was developing stalker tendencies.

The coffee was nice and started to clear the cobwebs from his brain. He leaned against the counter in his kitchen and looked out the glass doors into his backyard. A vivid picture of Jayde out there filled his mind. She would fill his house with the things it seemed to be lacking; laughter and color.

Setting down the coffee cup he was holding, Parker picked up the phone and called his father.

When Jayde went back down to the shop after her break, she felt better. She practiced some of her yoga breathing techniques and managed to calm herself down quite a bit.

Connor was behind the counter and gave Jayde a big smile when she walked in.

"Hey," Jayde smiled in return and gave him a quick hug, before asking, "What are you doing here?"

Connor tilted his head toward the kitchen, "Joe said I could come in and help out if I wanted to."

Jayde turned around and looked at Joe. He was filling an order and not looking at her. She smiled at him and then looked back at Connor, "Well, let's get these people all filled up before our friend, Harvey, decides to make his appearance.

The weather people were saying that Harvey's initial impact would be southwest of the Houston area, but he would stall out and then come back with a lot of rain. The Mayor of Houston was giving directions to residents and everyone seemed to take it in stride.

By the time the afternoon hit, the shop was filled up. Mostly people were talking about Harvey and checking in with their neighbors. Joe announced that they would open up on Saturday morning as long as the shop wasn't flooded. He made sure to have a backup generator installed when he renovated the shop. Everyone made an agreement that they would meet up there, to touch base.

When they closed up the shop, Jayde was bone-tired. It was a good day but she knew from experience, that this would just be the beginning.

Joe made sure to have an order of supplies delivered so they wouldn't run out of things.

It amazed Jayde with how prepared he was. When most people, her included, were going a little nutty with nerves, Joe was steady. Jayde assumed it was his intense training in the Marine Corps and she was appreciative of it.

Parker walked back into his house and sat down on the sofa in his living room. His neighbor, an elderly widow, asked him to help her with her plants. She was an avid gardener and was worried that the rain expected would harm her plants. She was kind enough to let him pick some of the flowers for Jayde so it was the least he could do.

Looking over, Parker noticed he had some messages.

One was from his parents, inviting him over for dinner. The second was from Owen. His assistant was going out of town to avoid the hurricane. And the last one was from Jayde. She said she missed him.

Dialing her number, Parker was smiling.

"Hello there," Jayde spoke into her phone when she saw that it was Parker. "How are you holding up?"

Still smiling, because that's what the sound of Jayde's voice did to him, Parker answered, "Better now that I'm talking to you."

'He's such a sweet-talker,' Jayde thought to herself. "Me too," She told him. "Work started out rough but by the end, I was fine."

Concerned, Parker asked her, "Are you really worried about the hurricane?"

"It's funny," Jayde explained, "I'm not really that worried about the storm itself, it's more about how things can change so quickly." She sighed, "You know, we're all chugging along fine, and then, Wham!"

Parker knew what she was saying, and it made him ache for her. "Are you sure I can't come and get you?"

Every time he asked her that, Jayde felt a little worse for turning him down. "I'd love to, but I already promised Joe I'd help out tomorrow."

Nodding, Parker felt a twinge of jealousy, and then silently chastised himself. He was new to Jayde's life. Joe and the shop were her family. It was unreasonable of him to expect her to drop all that she knew and loved just for him.

Not wanting to get bogged down in a conversation that would make her sad, Jayde asked, "So, where were you when I called earlier?"

Parker knew she was redirecting, and he was glad. "I was helping my neighbor. You know, the one who allowed me to pick those flowers for you." He got up and walked to the sliding door. "She's worried that the amount of rain they're calling for will hurt her flowers."

Jayde smiled. "That was sweet of you," She told him. It was easy to love him, because he was so sweet.

"Not really," Parker replied, "I just wanted to repay the favor."

'And he's also humble,' Jayde thought to herself. "I think it was just you being you."

Her words warmed Parker's insides and he wanted her more than ever. And, he wasn't even sure how that was possible. "Jayde, I think there's something I need to tell you." He began saying.

Jayde was about to answer when there was a knock on her door. "Parker, can I call you back, someone's knocking?"

Disappointed, Parker answered, "Uh, sure, no problem. Good night."

Still confused by Parker's abrupt end to their call, Jayde tucked her phone into her pocket and walked over to the door. She opened it up, and was shocked to find her friend, Felicia, there. "Hey sweetie," Jayde greeted her, and stepped aside to allow her friend inside. "What are you doing here?" She asked Felicia.

Felicia smiled, "I know that you stayed with my family during Ike, so I'm here to invite you over to my place while Harvey throws his temper tantrum."

Giggling, Jayde replied, "Boy, I'm getting all sorts of offers this time around."

Looking puzzled, Felicia asked, "And who else is trying to steal you away?"

Sitting down on the ottoman, Jayde motioned for her friend to take the oversized chair, before explaining. "You know the man I've been seeing? Parker?"

Nodding, and getting giddy with excitement, Felicia sat down. "I know he sounds awesome," She whispered, and waited.

"He is," Jayde said matter-of-factly, "He wanted me to go up and wait out the storm with him."

Making a show of looking around, Felicia frowned, before saying, "Um, and why are you here talking to me instead of snuggling up in his arms while a hurricane rages outside?"

It was same question Jayde was asking herself. She was afraid the answer wasn't going to make herself very happy. "I promised Joe I'd be here to help out."

Felicia took a moment to think about the statement, before answering. "I think Joe is great, the man really made a difference in your life," she paused, "but Parker is a chance at happiness."

Her friend was saying what Jayde knew in her heart, but had been unwilling to admit before now. "He is," She said flatly.

"Then what's the big question here?" Felicia asked her.

Jayde felt ashamed. She'd been fighting all of her feelings for Parker when she preached for years about embracing love and life. "I can't." She whispered, almost tripping over the words.

Felicia reached over and took her friends hand, giving it a light squeeze of reassurance. "Okay, listen, Lord knows I'm no expert on love." She smiled, "But let me ask you this, do you think that Parker feels for you what you feel for him?"

Of this, Jayde was clear. "Yes," She said adamantly. There was no way this was just one of them.

"Okay, then let me ask you this," Felicia took a breath before asking, "How long do you think another woman would wait to snatch him up if you keep pushing him away?"

The question made Jayde's head shoot up. She hadn't really thought about the situation in those terms. Felicia was being logical. If she didn't want Parker, or he thought she didn't want him, it wouldn't take long for someone else to come in and show him how much he was wanted. "Good point," She replied.

Smiling again, Felicia stood up. "I'll tell you what, you go up and spend a few days with him, and you let me know how much you're fighting anything after that." She winked at her friend and went to the door. "Please call me in a day or two so I know you made it through okay."

Following her friend to the door, Jayde smiled. "You have an uncanny way of putting things into perspective."

Hugging Jayde, Felicia made a small sound of doubt, and then said, "It's my lot in life, seeing the best for others and not having the faintest idea of what to do for myself."

"Well, I love you for it," Jayde told her.

Felicia waved and went downstairs. Jayde stood at the railing and waited for her friend to get to the entryway. She saw Joe come in and greet Felicia before she went back into her apartment.

Once inside her apartment, Jayde threw herself into the oversized chair Felicia just vacated. She closed her eyes, and let the thoughts of Parker flood into her mind. Him coming into the shop that first time, them going out to dinner, that first kiss, and finally realizing that she was in love with him. Within a few minutes, Jayde drifted off into a lovely sleep.

Parker decided to take his parents up on their dinner invitation. He felt a little neglected by Jayde and knew it was ridiculous. They were adults and both had a lot going on in their lives right now.

As he pulled into his parents' driveway, he was surprised to see them outside waiting. Giving them a suspicious look, Parker got out and walked up to meet them. "Mom," Parker smiled, "Dad, is there something going on?" He asked them.

Looking a little guilty, Glenn admitted, "She got it out of me."

Parker was torn between laughing at his father's apparent weakness in holding a secret and frowning at the pointed look his mother was shooting at him. "What?" He asked her, trying to sound innocent.

"That didn't work when you were six, and it isn't working now," Silvia replied. She leaned up and gave her son a kiss on the cheek. "Let's go inside and have dinner."

The three of them went inside. Parker felt a little like he was being led into an interrogation, but he tried to remember that his mother and father only wanted him to be happy. It only made the impending conversation slightly less stressful.

Once they were all seated, Silvia asked Glenn, "Can you please say Grace?"

Nodding, Glenn took his wife's hand and reached across to hold Parker's hand. It was these moments that gave him great joy.

Parker gave his mother some credit, she waited until they were eating before she started asking the questions.

"So," Silvia began, "Your father tells me that you've asked him for your grandmother's ring."

It was more of a statement than a question and, even anticipating it, Parker still felt uncomfortable. "Yes, I did." He replied, and then asked, "Is there an issue with that?" He wanted to make sure his mother knew he was confident. "Grandmother said it was for me."

Silently, Silvia was noting all the inflections in her son's words. It made her happy, but of course she couldn't let him know that. Not yet, anyway.

"Mom," Parker decided that he would take the questions she would invariably ask, off the table. "I love Jayde, I don't know how it happened so fast, and I don't know how I know it, I just do." He put his fork down and looked at his mother, "I asked Dad for the ring because when I finally get up the nerve, I'm going to ask her to marry me." He cleared his throat. "And, I want you both to be happy for me but I'm doing this because it's something I want."

Silvia had to dab her eyes with her napkin. It was a scary thing, when you heard your child be an adult. "I understand, and I just want to say that both your father and I are deliriously happy for both you and Jayde." She didn't want to make it too easy for him though, and added. "Of course, it would be nice if we met her before the wedding."

Glenn started chuckling, and winked his support to his son.

Parker figured that was about the extent of the conversation. He nodded, "It's a deal," he told her, and then asked, "So, have you been getting ready for this hurricane everyone has been talking about?"

When Jayde woke up, her neck was stiff. She didn't know how long she slept, she just knew it was late. Mr. Beethoven was curled up beside her on the chair, content. She hated to disturb him, but she had to move.

After she extricated herself from the chair, leaving a disgruntled Mr. Beethoven still in it, she went into the bathroom to get ready for bed. Looking at her phone, she saw it was well after twelve, and way too late to call Parker. Regret filled her heart.

Why did this keep happening? Why did she let every insecurity get in the way of her relationship with Parker? It was ridiculous, and annoying as hell.

As she was ready to get into bed, Jayde realized how loud it was outside. The wind had certainly picked up since she fell asleep. Since Joe put up the plywood up, it was impossible to see outside. All she could do was speculate about the storm outside. The metaphor wasn't lost on her either, it matched the "not knowing" she was feeling about Parker.

Her heart heavy, Jayde got into bed and prayed that Parker was safe, and that they would figure this all out.

Chapter 15

Saturday morning, Jayde woke up with her alarm, and felt a little disoriented. Joe actually put a sign up saying that the shop wouldn't open until eight a.m. instead of the regular six a.m. That meant that Jayde had an additional two hours to sleep and it didn't seem enough. She knew it was the internal storm inside of her, but she'd blame it on Harvey for right now.

When she went downstairs, Jayde didn't see Joe. On a hunch she walked over to the shop, and saw the lights on already. She knocked and smiled when he came to let her in. The wind was blowing wildly, but she couldn't see any damage anywhere around.

As Joe let her inside, Jayde greeted him warmly with, "Good morning, did you sleep?"

After receiving his non-committal shrug, Jayde guessed that he hadn't slept that well. "I did sleep, but the wind was raging."

Joe was ahead of her, going back to the kitchen, "Yeah, it was pretty bad out there." He pointed up to the television screen, "The Corpus Christi area was hit hard, but we just got a glancing blow."

Relief poured through Jayde. "I'm sorry for those who were affected but relieved that it wasn't that bad for us."

Joe nodded, "Some of the island had power outages but it looks like everyone is okay." He pointed toward the counter full of muffins. "Why don't you start putting those out front and we'll hand them out as people start trickling in."

Smiling, Jayde leaned over and gave Joe a quick kiss on the cheek. "You're a sweet guy, Joe," She told him as she grabbed a tray of muffins.

Joe called out after her, "Hey, don't let that get around."

Jayde was still smiling minutes later when the first customers showed up at the door. She said a final prayer for Parker, and went over to open the door.

Parker woke up in increments. Sleep was illusive for most of the night. When he finally fell into the abyss, dreams kept his mind going.

Coffee was definitely needed.

He turned on the television to watch the first reports of the hurricane.

No matter what was going on, and who was affected, it always tugged at his heart. Someone, somewhere was going through hell, having lost their home or business or both. He was glued to the news when his phone went off. It was his mom, asking him if he was okay. He replied quickly and went back to watching the news.

Jayde was ready for a break mid-morning. They were swamped. People were coming in, reporting the local damage, which thankfully wasn't much. Everyone was watching the news. At some point the night before, Joe installed a second television in the shop so all the customers could see the screens.

It was relief, but stress, all balled up inside of everyone. There was talk of getting together supplies and taking them down the coast to Rockport, Texas, where the hurricane made its landfall. Jayde was proud of the people she knew wanting to help others.

Joe came out of the kitchen and gave her a nod that said, "go on break." Jayde wasted no time, and went upstairs. There was no use in staying in the shop, she'd just get sucked back into the conversations the customers were having.

As she walked up the stairs, she dialed Parker's number. He answered quickly, with a breathy, "Hello."

Jayde briefly wondered if that was how he would sound in the morning, after they'd made love all night long. She sure hoped so. "Good morning," She returned.

Parker made a mental note that she sounded good. "How is it there?"

Smiling, Jayde replied, "Busy, but good. No major damage. A few power outages, but nothing too bad."

Although he was relieved, Parker still held onto a small bit of envy that she was there, and not with him. "Us too, nothing too bad."

Hope filled his chest. "Well then, do you think that Joe can spare you for a day or two?"

Oh, Jayde wished it was that easy. She would love to tell Joe, "I'm leaving for Parker's place," but it wasn't possible. Joe told Connor to stay home so it was just him at the shop. "I want to come up by you, it's just," She didn't get a chance to finish before Parker finished the sentence with, "Joe needs you."

Jayde could hear the resentment in his voice. "I'm sorry, Parker."

"I know you are," Parker started, and then, for some reason, he changed tact, "But I'd like to be as important to you as the shop."

Shocked by the words, and his tone, Jayde didn't know how to respond. This wasn't the sensitive and giving man, she thought Parker was. "First of all," Jayde tried to keep the anger out of her voice, "You are as important as the shop."

Feeling berated wasn't good. Parker knew he'd hit a nerve with Jayde but his own frustration was taking over. "I don't think so." He said with sarcasm, "I think you hide behind your responsibility so you don't have to do it."

"Do what?" Jayde almost shouted.

His own anger taking root, Parker shot out, "Fall in love, and take a chance."

Completely offended, and pissed, Jayde couldn't contain her own biting tone. "I'll tell you what, Parker Kinley, you have a lot of nerve saying something like that to me." She tried to calm herself, but it was too late now. "Fall in love, already done," She shouted, "But as far as taking a chance, why should I?" It was hard to keep the tears from falling as she spoke. "Why should I take that chance with a man who's so insecure he can't understand why I would want to help out a man who basically gave me the security and family I lost when my mother died?"

Parker could hear the hurt in her voice, and shame filled his gut. "Jayde, I," he started to apologize but she cut him off.

"Don't!" Jayde was yelling. "Good bye, Parker," She said, very calmly, and disconnected the call.

Parker stood in the kitchen of his house, and realized he just made the biggest mistake of his life.

Jayde cried for another ten minutes. She placed a cold washcloth on her eyes, trying to get the swelling down. It was obvious that she'd been crying, but she hoped no one noticed.

After she looked at Joe, a few minutes later, she knew he saw through her façade. Everyone else might have been preoccupied with the news and the situation, but Joe seemed to notice everything. Giving him a shrug, that told him she was "okay," Jayde put her apron back on and got to work helping customers.

Being busy was a double-edged sword to Jayde's way of thinking. It was nice to have time where Parker didn't fill her mind. But then, when things slowed down, wham; her thought were all about him. She was sweeping up the floor and their conversation replayed like a broken record. After mopping, she started crying because she couldn't believe he'd said those things to her. Hadn't she admitted she loved him? Hadn't she made time for him? So, she couldn't leave work, and helping people, for him, how was that so bad?

Joe stood in the doorway that led to the kitchen, and watched Jayde. Oh, that boy did something to make her mad. And Joe had a good mind to give Parker a piece of his mind about it. He considered himself Jayde's protector. A job that was serious, since he didn't have a child of his own. And, it wasn't like he hadn't fallen in love himself. When he was young, and new in the Marine Corps, there was a young woman who turned him upside down. When he got deployed, they couldn't even say goodbye. It still hurt, even two decades later. But still, he couldn't understand why that Parker kid would hurt Jayde. After watching Jayde take out her frustration on an unsuspecting mop, Joe decided to step in. "Hey Jayde," He grumbled as he walked over to her. "Why don't we just put everything up and call it a day."

Giving Joe a sigh on resignation, Jayde finally nodded, and said, "Okay, Joe."

They locked up and walked the short distance to the door that led upstairs to the apartments.

Jayde could feel her phone vibrating in her pocket but refused to answer it. If it was Parker, then she had absolutely nothing to say to him.

Joe diligently locked the entry door behind them and followed Jayde upstairs. She gave him a small wave when they reached the landing for his apartment. "You know," He said as he got out his key, "You're mad at him now for being stupid." Clearing his throat, and feeling more than a little uncomfortable giving out relationship advice, "But you'll forgive him because that's what love is about."

Again, Joe surprised Jayde. His wisdom spoke of someone who'd been in love but Jayde never once saw him even look twice at a woman. "Joe," She let her curiosity give her enough gumption to ask him, "Is t-hat where you go when you leave the shop for your break? Is there a woman out there who has your heart?"

Although Joe cared for Jayde, and looked at her as a daughter, he wasn't willing to talk about certain things. "I'm an old man, set in my ways," He grumbled, hoping that would keep her from asking more questions.

Giving Joe a nod, Jayde smiled. "I see," She replied. "Well, goodnight."

Joe waited until he heard Jayde's door close and lock before going all the way into his own apartment. Her questions made him think of things that happened a long time ago. And thinking about those things made him want to get out a bottle of whiskey and drown his sorrows.

Parker was pacing. He was glad that there wasn't carpet in his living room because it would have been worn through. As soon as Jayde ended their phone call, he knew he'd screwed up. Hell, he knew it before then; as soon as she said those stupid words about her not making him feel important. What the hell was wrong with him? He wasn't an insecure child, yet that's exactly what he acted like.

For some reason he couldn't even fathom, he'd said those words to get a response. It was completely irrational and he couldn't explain why, even hours later.

He'd called Jayde about a dozen times but didn't have the guts to actually leave a message. And now, it was getting later and later and his desperation was getting more severe.

Hurricane Harvey wasn't helping either. The damn hurricane was now dumping rain on them like it was some story out of the bible. The weather forecasters had warned people about this, but living it was something else altogether.

Finally, Parker decided to try and get some sleep.

He walked around the house, making sure everything was secure. He'd stop periodically and wonder how Jayde would think about a certain piece of furniture, or just stare out a window with her on his mind. It was maddening; knowing you hurt someone so much with some words. He decided to text her and at least say he was sorry....

Jayde, I know I was an ass. I can't explain why I said those stupid things, but I did. I love you.

Jayde was getting ready for bed when her phone went off. She read Parker's text and broke down into tears. She knew that he was sorry, but he'd said those words in the first place. After thinking about it for hours, Jayde realized that he was, on some level, right. She was scared. She was damn scared. What if it didn't work out? What if she wasn't good enough for him?

Sitting up, Jayde realized that was the crux of her fears, not being good enough.

She picked up the phone and dialed Sister Margaret's number. The phone was ringing and Jayde was praying it wasn't too late.

Margaret picked up on the third ring, "Hello, Jayde, are you okay?" She asked.

Still crying, Jayde said, "No, I'm in love."

It was tough not to laugh when someone made such a statement in the most pitiful tone ever. "Usually, it's been my experience that falling in love is a good thing." She smiled, "You make it seem like a noncommunicable disease."

"Ha ha," Jayde retorted in a flat voice. "Isn't it though?" She was being a sap, she knew it. "It's just that Parker said some pretty hurtful things earlier today and it's eating away at me."

The situation was becoming clearer to Margaret. "Ahhh, so you're in a tormented state not exactly about what he said, but that whatever he said had some ring of truth."

"You know, you should take that show to Vegas, you're psychic," Jayde said.

Clearing her throat, Sister Margaret frowned. "Choose your words a little more carefully, Jayde. I love you, but I still require the respect I've earned."

Now Jayde smiled. Leave it to Sister Margaret to put her in her place so succinctly. "I apologize Sister," Jayde mumbled. "You're right." She sighed. "He said I was too afraid to fall in love and take a chance. He was mad because he wanted me to ride out the storm up at his place."

"Why didn't you go?" Margaret asked.

Tears began falling again. "Because Joe needed me at the shop."

Making a sound of displeasure, Margaret responded, "In all the years I've known Joe, I never knew that he couldn't possibly run the shop without you."

A new layer of guilt piled up in Jayde's chest.

"Did Joe actually ask you to stay at the shop, knowing that Parker wanted you to go up to his house?" Margaret asked. She knew the answer already, but she was trying to help her young friend come to the realization herself.

Jayde ran her fingers through her hair, "Uh, no, he didn't know that Parker asked me to go." She wanted to give her reasons for not going, and said, "But Joe gave me the home and security I needed after losing mom, and I couldn't just desert him."

Margaret shook her head. "Do you think Joe would feel deserted if you went up to Parker's house, during a hurricane?" She took a breath. "You don't think that Joe would understand being in love and wanting to spend a stressful time with those we love?"

Not able to answer, due to the ball of guilt clogging her throat, Jayde simply gave a non-committal, "Mmm."

"That's not an answer, young lady," Sister Margaret used her best "mom" voice.

A tear slid down Jayde's cheek, "No, ma'am," she answered. "He said I didn't make him feel important." She didn't want to whine, but the words came out that way.

Margaret shook her head, she knew the words would hurt Jayde. "You didn't, it's that simple." She wanted to reassure Jayde though, so she followed up with, "But it's something you can fix, Jayde." She smiled, "You are one of the most loving people I know. You have this wonderful way of viewing life, and you deserve someone who recognizes that trait. From what you've told me, Parker does."

"Yes," Jayde managed to whisper.

Her smile wider now, Margaret said, "So why are you talking to me and not telling Parker how wonderful he is and how important he is to you and that you'll be happy to go up there to see him tomorrow."

Hope began to bubble up in Jayde's chest. "Do you think he'll forgive me?" She asked.

Chuckling, Sister Margaret asked in return, "How many times has he called you since your argument?"

"About a dozen," Jayde replied, and chuckled herself.

Sitting down on her bed, Sister Margaret looked at a picture she kept of herself and the young priest she shared a brief love with. "So, don't waste any more time fighting, Jayde. Lord knows, life is too short. Losing your mother should have taught you that." She wanted to encourage Jayde. "And tell him how much you appreciate that he brought this to your attention and how you'll work on it. But you'll need to ask him for more patience."

Jayde nodded, "Well, he's not the only one who could use some patience right about now."

"Lord knows we all do," Sister Margaret told Jayde, and felt better about their conversation. "Now, you hang up with me and call him."

Jayde's smile was full-blown now. "I will, thank you," She paused, "And Sister?" She asked.

Margaret waited, "Yes," she replied.

Jayde took a breath, and then admitted, "That young man you loved, I'm sure he's still wondering if he made the right decision."

Not wanting to comment, Margaret just said, "Only he and the Lord know, goodnight sweetie."

"Good night," Jayde whispered, and hung up the phone.

Jayde waited a few minutes to compose herself, and then called Parker's phone. She frowned when it went right to voicemail, but decided to leave a message for him. "Parker, I'm so sorry we fought. I know you're right on some levels. I do love you. Call me."

Chapter 16

Parker dozed off on the sofa. He woke up when there was a knock on his front door. Getting up, he wiped the sleep from his eyes and made his way to the door. When he opened it up, he found his neighbor, Mrs. Jenkins, standing there.

"Parker," Mrs. Jenkins said softly, "I'm so sorry to bother you but I'm having trouble getting my garage door to shut. I didn't realize I left it open until Mrs. Waller, from down the street, called to tell me."

Smiling, Parker nodded, and told her, "Don't worry about it, I'll help you with it." He closed the door behind him, and walked Mrs. Jenkins back to her house.

It was two in the morning, and Jayde was wide awake. Parker hadn't called her back and she was devastated. She could logically understand him being upset with her, but it hurt deeply that he didn't call her back.

The wind had picked up again and she could hear the rain pelting the window. Felicia texted her an hour earlier to say how much rain they were getting at her apartment complex. Jayde prayed that her friend would be spared from the onslaught of rain the weather forecasters were predicting.

She finally decided to turn on the television, even though she knew it wouldn't be good.

Sure enough, Houston was flooding. They were having reports of flooding in the areas surrounding the city too. Already there were television crews filming people being rescued from their flooding homes. Jayde cried for them.

Parker managed to help his neighbor with her garage door. It took a good hour, and the help of another neighbor, but they got it working. After he came home, he fell onto his bed, still clothed, and fell asleep.

He woke up, not knowing what woke him, but knowing it was worrisome. There was the sound of water, and Parker thought he must have washed his hands and left the water running in his bathroom. As soon as his feet moved to the floor, he was corrected.

Water was in his house, running along the floor like a stream. It was past his ankles now and almost had a current, the way it was pulling against him as he was trying to walk.

Not panicking, Parker was more worried about his neighbor, Mrs. Jenkins. She would not do well with water in her house.

As Parker was walking into the living room, he did a double take. Since the back of his living room had huge glass doors, he was able to see the water rushing up his yard. It was like a weird dream. He knew he should get out, but it was fascinating to watch. As he tried to figure out what to do, his foot kicked something. He reached down and picked up his phone. It must have dropped on the floor last night when he answered the door. "Well, crap!" He muttered.

Wading through his house, Parker went back into his bedroom and grabbed a small safe he kept in his closet. It was small enough that he could lift, and he placed it up on a top shelf. If the house had water, he was pretty sure his car was toast and undriveable. Now it was a matter of getting to higher ground.

Within ten minutes of waking up, Parker saw the water rise up about six inches. Time was becoming desperate. He grabbed a jacket and waded to the front door.

Looking down the street, Parker saw that half the neighborhood was flooded. Some of his neighbors were already making their way down the street, towards higher ground.

Parker worked his way through the water to Mrs. Jenkins house. He pounded on the door, and yelled, "It's Parker, Mrs. Jenkins, I'm here to help."

Listening closely, Parker thought he could hear something from inside. Looking around, he found a good-sized flower plant. Yelling again, he said, "I'm going to break your window, and come inside."

He stopped for just a second to listen for any noise. Again, he could hear something faint.

With as much momentum as he could get, Parker swung the flower pot and turned his head just as the pot made contact with the window. The glass shattered, and he used his shirt to pull out the large shards. Once he was able to get through the window, he started calling, "Mrs. Jenkins!"

Between the sound of the torrential rain, and the sound the water was making as it was filling the house, Parker couldn't hear anything. He waded through the water that was now up past his knees. "Mrs. Jenkins," He kept calling as he made his way through the house.

He'd only ever been in the entryway of Mrs. Jenkins' house so he wasn't sure of the layout. Certain that the master bedroom was toward the rear of the house, Parker made his way there.

Opening up a closed door, he called out once more, "Mrs. Jenkins!"

There was a noise to his right.

When Parker looked over, he was shocked. A tree had fallen through the roof and was blocking another door. He listened carefully and could hear Mrs. Jenkins say, "Parker."

Having no clue as to how long she'd been in there, Parker's main concern was getting her out. The water was rising and he had no idea if she was trapped and could drown. Most of the branches were small enough that he could pull them away. A very large branch was blocking the door. Parker yelled, "There's a large branch here, I'm going to try to move it, okay?"

There was a faint, "Okay."

Parker had no idea how long it took him to move that branch. He didn't dare leave to try and find help. Fear clawed at his insides now. "I'm almost there," He would shout out every few minutes so Mrs. Jenkins knew he was still fighting to free her.

What seemed like hours, but was probably only minutes, Parker had cleared enough branches to wedge the door open. He peeked inside and could see Mrs. Jenkins. She was perched on top of a large dresser she had in her closet. "I can see you, I'm going to get the door opened, but you're going to have to come here and squeeze through."

"I'm scared," Mrs. Jenkins told him. She was relieved that someone found her, but she couldn't swim and was very afraid of the water.

Parker smiled, "Mrs. Jenkins," he told her, "I'm right here and I'm not leaving without you."

Crying now, Mrs. Jenkins wiped the tears from her cheeks, "My dear husband used to say things like that."

Smiling, Parker replied, "Well, he's here with us right now. I'm sure he's the one who told me to come over and check on you."

Mrs. Jenkins nodded, "I'm sure of it." She gingerly got down off the dresser. She gasped when she put her feet in the water."

By now, Parker could reach his hand into the closet. "Take my hand," He instructed her.

Once he felt her hand grasp his, Parker started to wedge the door open further. It wouldn't open fully so she would have to squeeze through it. "You've got it, just push through as I push the door open."

"I should have lost that last twenty pounds," Mrs. Jenkins said through gritted teeth as she tried to get through the partially opened door.

With a small chuckle, Parker retorted, "You're beautiful, I'm sure your husband felt like the luckiest man in the world." He hoped his attempt at distracting her would help her through this. The water was up to his thighs now and the situation was becoming more dangerous.

Finally squeezing through the opening, Mrs. Jenkins flung herself into Parker's arms. "Thank you," She whispered into his ear.

Wanting to comfort his neighbor, but knowing they weren't in the clear yet, he instructed her, "Okay, we've got to get out of here. I need you to stay right behind me." He turned so he could lead them, "Hold my shirt in your hands and don't let go, okay?"

With a shaky, "Okay," Mrs. Jenkins followed his directions.

It was slow going, but they made it to the front door. It would be too difficult to open the large door, so Parker helped her go through the window.

Parker made sure she was safely outside the house before going through the window himself.

He just reached Mrs. Jenkins, when he swept her up into his arms. "It's easier if I carry you."

Even with the rain pelting down on them, Mrs. Jenkins managed to give him a smile.

They made it halfway through the yard when they heard a noise.

Parker turned and saw a boat coming toward them. Relief flooded through him.

The boat pulled up beside them and two men reached out, saying, "We'll take this lovely lady off your hands."

Nodding, Parker helped lift Mrs. Jenkins up into the boat. Then it was his turn. The men had to practically pull him in, he didn't realize how tired he was.

Within a minute, the boat started up and they were taken about a mile down the street.

There were jacked up trucks waiting at an intersection that hadn't flooded. People were offering blankets and trying to get names of those who needed medical care.

An off-duty nurse looked over them. She listened to Mrs. Jenkins describe what happened. When it was Parker's turn, she told him, "You're a hero."

Shaking his head, Parker replied, "No ma'am, you are." And he thought of Jayde. Suddenly everything she'd been telling him made sense. How important it was to help people. How even the smallest thing like a blanket, or a cup of coffee, or simply a warm smile can help someone deal with the craziness of life. His heart felt very heavy.

Jayde was still glued to her television when there was a knock on her apartment door. For a brief moment, she thought it might be Parker but the news was saying that the 45 Freeway was flooded and impassable.

She got up and found Joe at her door. "Are we opening?" She asked him.

With a quick nod, Joe responded, "Yeah, I'm sure that someone needs a cup off coffee or one of my world-famous muffins."

The way he said the words, Jayde had to laugh. "Okay then," She smiled, "Give me about twenty minutes."

Joe gave her a quick wave and left to go downstairs.

A few minutes later, Jayde was braiding her hair and willing her phone to ring. She wanted to hear from Parker and know that he was okay.

Jayde kept her promise and was downstairs in exactly twenty minutes. Wrapping her apron around her waist, she told Joe, "Well, I sure hope there are people who need a cup of coffee and a world-famous muffin."

Joe shot her a dry look.

As if on cue, the Senior Three Amigos came into the shop.

Gretchen was first, and shouted, "Coffee! I need coffee!"

Ginny called out, "A muffin please!"

Laughing, Jayde looked at Joe and broke into laughter. It was a wonderful relief, getting the break from the stress of the last couple of days. She was still worried about Parker and what would go on with them, but this moment, spent laughing, was what she needed.

Ray came up to the counter, and smiled at Jayde. "How are you holding up?" He asked.

Sighing, Jayde replied, "We're fine, but I've been watching the news and it's heartbreaking."

"All we can do is hope that people are safe," Ray assured her.

'Truer words were never spoken,' Jayde thought to herself. She said a quick prayer for Parker and then pasted a smile on her face when more customers came into the shop.

Parker woke up and was disoriented. Him and some of his neighbors were taken to a local school for the day. He managed to get a few hours of sleep and now, the severity of the last day was overwhelming.

Mrs. Jenkins sat down beside him and handed him a cup filled with coffee. "Did you get some sleep?" She asked.

Nodding, Parker responded, "I did, and woke up not remembering where I was."

Giving Parker a warm smile, Mrs. Jenkins rubbed her eyes quickly. "They aren't letting us go back to check on the damage until it's safe." She took a deep breath, "I'm going to stay with my sister near Austin for a few days."

It was something Parker needed to consider. He didn't even have his phone or his wallet.

As if reading his mind, Mrs. Jenkins offered, "They're letting people borrow phones to call their families. Why don't you go and call your parents?"

Getting up, Parker felt stiff. All the trauma of their situation was catching up with him now. He slowly made his way over to where there was a table with volunteers. Waiting in line, he wanted to call Jayde, but couldn't remember her number. As soon as she'd called him, he put it in his phone and didn't pay attention to the actual number.

When it was his turn, he dialed his mother's number. She answered quickly, sounding upset. "Mom, I'm okay," He got out quickly before she bombarded him with questions. After giving her a very short explanation, he asked if she could pick him up.

An hour later, Silvia and Glenn were pulling up outside the school that was converted to a makeshift shelter. They parked and walked inside. It was chaotic, but people were calm.

Silvia found someone quickly and asked about their son. A volunteer showed them where people were waiting. As soon as Silvia saw Parker, she started crying. "Oh, thank the Lord," She whispered to her son.

Parker held onto his mother tightly. Even at his age, it was nice to have your parents there. "I'm okay," He repeated, and let go of her so he could hug his dad.

"Let's get you home," Glenn said, noticing some of the cuts and bruises on his son's face and arms.

It took them another hour before they were able to get to his parents' house. A lot of roads were still impassible and the rerouted cars were backed up.

Parker was dog-tired by the time they got into his parents' house. He turned down his mother's offer of food, and just went upstairs to his old room. He didn't even take off his clothes, just fell onto the bed, and went to sleep.

After she and Joe closed the shop, Jayde decided to try and call Parker. If he was mad, she could understand, but she just wanted to make sure he was okay. Unfortunately, his phone went straight to voicemail. For some reason, it made Jayde very nervous.

She was getting ready for bed, and watching the news again, when she almost jumped out of the chair she was sitting in. They were showing footage of some of the flooded neighborhoods, and there....on the screen, was Parker's house.

All of Jayde's insides were tossed about. Her heart was beating so fast, she thought it might beat out of her chest. Tears streamed down her cheeks. She whispered, "Lord, let him be okay."

Chapter 17

The next morning, Parker woke up because he was hungry. If memory served, he hadn't eaten in almost a day and a half, so it was no wonder his stomach was growling like a wild animal.

He took a shower and got dressed in some clothes he'd left in the room ages ago. Thank goodness, they still fit.

On a list of preferences, Parker knew talking to his parents wasn't high on the list, but they deserved to know he was okay.

Silvia and Glenn were sitting in the breakfast nook, discussing the hurricane and its aftermath. They felt lucky that they were not devastatingly affected by all the rain that fell. People like their son, lost their whole houses, and all their possessions. It was heartbreaking. When they saw Parker come into the room, they stopped discussing it.

"Good morning," Silvia said as she stood up and walked around the table to give her son a hug. "How are you feeling?" She asked him.

Tilting his head back and forth, Parker replied, "I'm okay. I slept well."

Glenn nodded, "I came in to check on you before we went to bed and you were out."

For some reason, Parker felt good about knowing his dad still checked up on him. "Thanks," He said to his dad.

Parker and his dad sat down while Silvia went over to the oven and took out a plate she was heating. She set it down in front of Parker and, seeing the look he shot her, told him, "Eat it!"

There was enough food on his plate to feed two or three people, but he knew his mom meant well, so he did his best to eat.

The three of them talked about what happened during the storm. He tried to downplay the whole thing in Mrs. Jenkins' house. His parents had enough to worry about.

Silvia listened, and tried not to cry. "Are you okay emotionally?" She asked her son.

"I don't think it's hit me yet," Parker answered. "When we go back, we'll judge what's got to be done."

Nodding, Silvia could understand that. "And what about Jayde?" She asked next. "I'm sure she was relieved that you're okay."

Feeling ashamed, Parker shook his head in denial.

Looking skeptical, she asked her son, "Haven't you called her to let her know you're okay?"

Parker looked from his mother, to his father, and back to his mother. All the emotions he was feeling were multiplied, "I lost my phone and I don't know her number." He tried not to sound like a kid in trouble.

Silvia gave her son her most practiced "mom look," and asked, "Uh, you know where she works right? Don't you think that if you asked her boss that you couldn't get ahold of her?"

In that moment, Parker knew he wasn't even thinking straight. "You've got a point, mom," He commented, then was very interested in his food.

Folding her arms across her chest, Silvia did her best not to laugh. She shot her husband a look, and he was preoccupied with the food left on his plate. She could tell from his demeanor that he was trying to keep a straight face as well.

"After you're done eating, go into my office and use the phone," She announced as she started clearing dishes off the table.

Fifteen minutes later, Parker was sitting at his mother's desk, staring at the phone.

What did he say? What could he say?

Sitting there for a while, he wondered if Joe would even take his call. For that matter, would Joe pass on the message if Jayde wasn't there?

Hearing a noise, Parker looked up and saw his mom. She'd poked her head in the door.

Giving her son a pointed look, Silvia spoke sternly, and said, "You'll never know how she feels until you speak to her."

"Yes, mom," Parker replied.

He dialed the number.

Jayde was busy. Now that the storm was dying down, the weather turned cold and everyone seemed to need coffee.

There was a line outside when they opened the door and it hadn't stopped since. She appreciated the distraction since the only other thing she was doing was worrying about Parker. She'd tried his cell phone dozens of times and even tried calling his office, with no answer there either. She prayed he was okay.

The phone was ringing at the café and Joe grumbled, "I'll get it."

He answered it with a gruff, "Hello."

Parker could hear Joe's voice and his fear multiplied. "Um," He started, "Joe, this is Parker Kinley, is Jayde there?"

"She is," Joe snapped back at the young man, "but why should she talk to the likes of you?" His question was rhetorical, "She's busy right now."

Being brushed off like that was tough for Parker, "I understand," he said quietly, and then asked, "Could you please ask her to call me?"

Joe gave a grunt, and disconnected the call. He looked over the counter that separated the kitchen from the shop and frowned. He knew Jayde was an adult, and he knew she was worried about Parker. Obviously, the young man was okay because he just called, but Joe would have to think long and hard about passing on the message.

Jayde was beat! The day was a brutal one with customers coming in and out and focused on Harvey and his aftermath. She was addicted to watching the news at night and seeing all of the devastation day-after-day was wearing her down. She was trying to catch a glimpse of Parker, she knew that. She'd stopped leaving messages for him and prayed for his safety multiple times a day.

After saying goodnight to Joe, she went into her apartment and threw herself onto the bed.

Mr. Beethoven jumped up and purred as he tried to snuggle into her side. Jayde smiled, knowing it was his way of comforting her.

Her phone went off, and Jayde jumped up so fast that Mr. Beethoven jumped. He gave her a grumpy look before sauntering off. Jayde answered the call with a breathless, "Hello."

"Jayde," Trisha Headlan, said.

A smile crossed Jayde's face, and she asked, "Auntie Trisha?"

Trisha smiled in return. "Yes, it's me." She answered Jayde, and giggled. "I knew I had to call you, I'm so sorry it's been so long."

Already pushing the time aside, Jayde told her, "Oh, don't worry about that, I'm just so glad you called. I've been down."

Knowing her instincts were right, Trisha sighed. "I'm coming for a visit, is that okay?"

Surprised, but in a completely happy way, Jayde replied, "Of course, get your butt down here."

Laughing, Trisha told her, "Okay, let me give you my flight info. I'll rent a car and drive down from Hobby Airport."

"Okay," Jayde answered, feeling lighter emotionally for the first time in days.

Trisha didn't want to pry too much right now, but she told Jayde, "And you can tell me all about the man who is wreaking havoc in your life."

Chuckling, Jayde asked, "How did you know?"

With a sigh, Trisha explained, "Well, ninety-nine percent of the time, if a woman is down, it's a man who's behind it."

Still chuckling, Jayde said, "That sounds about right."

They stayed on the phone only long enough for Jayde to take down Trisha's travel information. Her mom's best friend would be down in two days.

After hanging up, Jayde wondered if she could hang on to her sanity long enough for reinforcements to arrive.

Parker woke up and just laid in bed. He knew he needed to get up but he didn't want to. Jayde didn't call him back. And, if that wasn't bad enough, he was going back to his house today with his parents to check out the damage. Mrs. Jenkins called him the night before and informed him that they had the go-ahead to check out the damage.

His house was important, but Parker found himself more preoccupied with Jayde and why she wouldn't call him back.

He was still laying there when his dad knocked, and told him, "Parker, we're leaving in thirty minutes."

"Okay, thanks," He called out. Deciding he needed to start figuring out what to do so he got out of bed.

The drive to his neighborhood was something out of a movie. The waters were receding but the damage they caused was immense. Driving past businesses and houses, Parker realized he wasn't alone in the confusion.

His dad pulled into the driveway of the house and they got out.

"I don't think I even locked it when I left," Parker informed his parents.

The three of them walked inside and stopped just inside the entryway.

It was total destruction.

One of the glass doors on to his patio was gone so the whole house was exposed to the elements. There was still about two inches of water on the floor.

They slowly made their way into the living room.

You could see where the water stopped, about four feet up the walls.

Parker just slowly turned and surveyed the damage.

Silvia saw the disbelief in her son's eyes, and walked over to hug him. "We'll figure it out," She told him.

Parker walked into the kitchen and made the mistake of opening the refrigerator. Since the power went out, everything in there was spoiled and the smell was atrocious. "Oh geez," He exclaimed, and closed the door.

Glenn was standing next to his wife, and staring at their son. He couldn't imagine walking into your house and seeing that it was a total loss. Looking at his wife, Glenn could see she was trying to hold back tears. He pulled her close to him.

Parker led the way as they explored the rest of the house. There wasn't one room that didn't take on water. It was like a river came through and then just left.

He walked into the garage and hit the door opener. As the rolling door went up, Parker could see that his car even took on water. It was most likely lost too.

Glenn put his hand on his son's shoulder, and asked, "Are you okay?"

Parker shrugged, "I don't know yet, let me get back to you."

Giving his son a small smile of encouragement, Glenn just nodded and followed Parker outside to the driveway.

They were standing there for only a few moments before they saw Mrs. Jenkins making her way over.

She gave them a friendly wave as she approached. "Hello there," She said when she was close enough.

Parker told her, "We just walked through the house, I think it's a total loss."

With a quick shrug, Mrs. Jenkins replied, "Yep, mine too."

Her reaction was puzzling to Parker. He commented, "You seem awfully calm about this."

With a nod, Mrs. Jenkins replied, "I guess I am." She turned to Parker's parents and said, "I want to thank you both for raising such a great man. He saved my life."

Silvia smiled, and looked from her son's neighbor to him. "He said you both left together."

Mrs. Jenkins shook her head at Parker. "I see he's humble as well. Why don't you walk with me a bit and I'll tell you a story," She took Silvia's arm and they walked away.

Parker and his father went back inside to see if they could salvage some clothes. He'd already called his insurance company and they said it could take up to a few weeks to get someone out. Parker started to take pictures of everything his could with a camera he borrowed from his dad. He still hadn't replaced his phone for some reason.

When his mother and Mrs. Jenkins got back to the house, Parker suspected that he was in a little bit of trouble with his mother. He just kept taking pictures.

Silvia stood outside with her husband, and allowed the tears to fall down her face. "Our boy could have died," She told Glenn.

Pulling his wife to him, Glenn whispered, "I know, but there is a different plan for him."

"Mrs. Jenkins showed me what he did, Glenn. It's a miracle neither of them was hurt worse." Silvia said, overwhelmed with emotions.

When Parker came out of the house, he smiled at his parents in an attempt to tell them he was okay. He realized, as he was walking through his house, that there wasn't much inside that he was troubled about losing. All of his important papers were in a safe, neatly tucked into the trunk of his parents' car. Everything else could be replaced.

"Ready?" He asked his parents.

Silvia and Glenn nodded.

They were going over to his office to try to make heads or tales of what damage was done there. Some of the areas in Friendswood, where his office was located, suffered flooding.

When they pulled up to the business center, Parker knew that there was water damage. Other business owners in the same complex were in the process of cleaning out their offices.

Parker got out of the car and was shocked to see Owen there already.

"What are you doing here?" Parker asked his assistant.

Owen smiled, "Well, I thought I'd help you out so you had to pay me."

Even Owen's smart-assed remarks were okay today. Parker asked, "You think so, huh?"

Shrugging, Owen retorted, "Well, if you don't, I see your mom right behind you, so I think I'm pretty well set."

Silvia laughed. She'd always liked Owen. He kept her son from getting too uptight. "Well Parker, I think he's got you there."

Rolling his eyes, Parker announced, "Okay, no more horsing around, let's get this done."

The four of them went into the office and got to work.

Jayde stood at the counter to the kitchen, and waited for Joe to hand her an order of food.

She was so tired.

The night before, she was cleaning her already-cleaned apartment to prepare for Aunt Trisha's arrival. Joe was nice enough to offer the use of the other studio apartment during Trisha's stay, but Jayde didn't know what her Aunt wanted to do.

With still no word from Parker, Jayde's nerves were frayed and her heart was smashed. She realized how in love with him she was, and now she was afraid she wouldn't get over it.

Joe handed her the plate, and commented, "You look tired, should probably take off early today."

Smiling at him, Jayde simply replied, "We'll see."

Jayde delivered the order to the customers, and went back behind the counter.

The shop was steady but not busy enough to keep the thoughts of Parker at bay.

She would talk to Aunt Trisha later and they would come up with a plan. Then again, how did one make a plan to heal one's heart?

Chapter 18

It was almost seven o'clock when Jayde's phone went off. She picked it up quickly, excitement flooding her heart. "Aunt Trisha, where are you?"

"Look out your window," Trisha answered.

Jayde ran over to the window. Now that Joe took down the plywood, the whole apartment felt better. She peeled back the curtains and looked down. There was Trisha, dressed in a bright, flowery dress, and waving.

Running down the stairs, Jayde was so happy. She needed to see a friendly face right now.

As she walked out onto the sidewalk, Jayde yelped in glee. "Oooooh, I'm so glad you're here," She said as she was enveloped into a warm hug.

"Me too," Trisha said into Jayde's hair. "It's been too long." She stepped back so she could look at Jayde. The girl was gorgeous, but it wasn't difficult to see the heartbreak in her. "Let's get upstairs so we can talk."

They made their way upstairs, chatting as they went.

Jayde was asking all sorts of questions. "How's L.A.?"

Trisha shrugged, "It's still there, or so I'm told. I live down near San Diego now."

With a frown, Jayde wondered why Aunt Trish didn't mention moving earlier.

As Jayde was showing Trisha inside the apartment, she heard Joe on the landing downstairs. She walked to the railing and leaned over, saying, "Joe, my aunt is here. I'll bring her down to the shop tomorrow to meet everyone."

A quick wave was Joe's only response. Jayde shook her head in wonder, and then went back into her apartment.

Trisha was already curled up on the oversized chair, and Mr. Beethoven was up on her lap, settling in and purring.

"I can't believe it, you just draw them in," Jayde commented as she walked into the kitchen area to make some tea.

Rolling her eyes, Trisha snorted. "Yes, cats; men, not so much."

Jayde giggled.

Slowly putting a reluctant Mr. Beethoven on the floor, Trisha got up and walked over to Jayde. "And your man, he's broken your heart."

The statement surprised Jayde. She hadn't mentioned Parker. "I guess he's not my man, and yes, he's crushed my heart."

Trisha nodded. "I'll help in any way I can." She did a slow turn in the room. "This apartment is adorable, how long have you been here?"

"Three years now, I think," Jayde answered. She lifted up two different teas and allowed Trisha to pick which one she wanted. "It's been too long since I've seen you," Trisha commented. "Your mother expected me to be there for you."

Thinking about her mother made Jayde smile. "You've always been there for me, and you knew when I had to figure stuff out for myself."

"But still," Trisha rushed.

Jayde led the way back over to the living room corner, and motioned for Trisha to take the chair. She sat down on the ottoman and crossed her legs in front of her. "There is no, "but still," Auntie Trisha, I have had a great life." She closed her eyes, and took a breath. "Correct that, I have a great life."

Trisha shook her head in astonishment. Seeing Jayde was like seeing Frannie twenty-five years earlier. A free spirit with a huge heart. "Your mom would be so proud of you," Trisha swiped at the tear that formed at the corner of her eye.

"I'd like to think so," Jayde responded, closing her eyes and thinking of her mother. "I've been afraid lately, and I think I pushed someone away."

With a nod, Trisha took a sip of her tea. When she put it back down, she asked, "Is this the someone who crushed your heart?"

All Jayde could do was nod.

Watching Jayde, Trisha couldn't help but smile. "I'll tell you what, let's discuss all the bad stuff tomorrow. Tonight, let's just talk about good stuff like movies, music, and food."

Laughing, Jayde nodded eagerly. "Oh, when you come into the shop tomorrow, prepare yourself for some great food."

"Oooh, you know these hips were made from chocolate," Trisha said flippantly.

They laughed and began talking about lighter things.

Parker was exhausted.

He'd spent the last couple of days talking to insurance companies, comparing notes with his neighbors, and trying to get a plan together for reassembling his life.

There were two suggestions and he didn't know what to do. Some suggested he just gut it all and start fresh while others suggested drying everything out and then seeing what was salvageable. Either way, it was a lot of work and he had both his house and his office to contend with. Not only that, but there was still no word from Jayde.

Every day that he didn't hear from her made it feel like he was moving farther and farther away from her. His mother suggested, on regular intervals, that he should quit being prideful and go down there. He'd messed up and she didn't forgive him. It made no sense to go down there and just get rejected again.

He was sitting out on his parents' patio when his father came out to join him.

Glenn Kinley looked at his son, and knew it was bad. "You don't hide it too well," He commented to Parker.

"What's to hide?" Parker asked his father.

Dropping his head, Glenn hesitated, and then looked at Parker. "Nothing, I misspoke. I meant to say that you looked like shit."

The words, coming from his father, was enough to give Parker pause. "Thanks, Dad," He said shortly.

Glenn stood up and began to pace. "Listen," He pointed at his son, "I've been quiet about what's going on since your life is basically up in the air."

Remorse was filling up Parker's chest. He didn't comment, only nodded.

"But, come on, man," Glenn lifted his hands, and dropped them in defeat, "If you love her, don't just toss it away."

Unwilling to listen, Parker stood up. He turned to his father, and said, "I appreciate you and Mom putting me up and the inconvenience of it, but I don't need your input on my love life." He walked into the house.

Glenn stood on the patio, shaking his head. It was a shame that young people weren't smarter. He gave his wife a half-smile when she came out to hug him.

"I know," Silvia said, "he's being a jerk."

Reluctantly, Glenn agreed, but said, "Although I would've used a more colorful description."

Smiling, Silvia sighed. "Well, I know you have a strict, 'we don't meddle,' policy but it may be unavoidable."

Releasing his hold on his wife, Glenn walked the length of the patio. He was always proud of the home he and Silvia built. He wanted that kind of love and pride for his boys. "For once," He turned to look at his wife, "you might be right about the meddling."

Silvia tried to cover up her surprise with a warm smile.

Jayde woke up just before her alarm went off. She was glad she did since she could silence it and try not to wake Aunt Trisha. They'd stayed up later than Jayde usually did, and talked about movies, music, and most especially about food. Aunt Trisha promised to make Jayde a dish her mother used to make for her when she was a little girl. Seeing Trisha was a double-edged sword; lovely because Jayde felt the bond they had, and sad because Trisha and her mother were so similar.

Doing some yoga stretches, without music, helped Jayde focus on getting going. Mr. Beethoven didn't even budge from his place on the bed next to Trisha. Jayde mouthed the word, 'traitor,' to him as she passed him.

Jayde managed to get out of the apartment without waking up Trisha, and that made her happy.

Joe was his usual chipper self, and they went down to the shop in relative silence.

About fifteen minutes later, Joe poked his head around the counter, and asked Jayde, "So did your friend make it in alright?"

Nodding, Jayde gave him a bright smile, "Oh yeah, we were talking about food, and I kept raving about yours."

A small blush wove its way into Joe's cheeks. "Yeah, yeah, you're just wanting a sample."

"Basically," Jayde grinned, "yes."

Joe shook his head and went back into the kitchen. Within thirty minutes though, Jayde was given a plate with a lot of samples. She was testing a particularly tasty croissant when Parker popped into her mind. He seemed to do that when her mind was open. Another double-edged sword for her to contend with.

Luckily it was time for the shop to open, so Jayde managed to tuck the thoughts of Parker away for the moment.

Parker woke up but stayed in bed. He did that every day now; just stayed there, thinking about Jayde mostly.

The insurance company got in touch with him earlier than he thought they would so that ball was rolling. The business was hashed out pretty quickly, and he was glad that he had the presence of mind to store all of his business data on the off-site server. He wasn't up and running yet but he told Owen they would get back to work soon.

What boggled his mind was how very surreal everything seemed now. His life was basically in limbo. And that wouldn't be so bad except that Jayde wasn't with him. He knew, if she were here, then he'd be okay. It hurt that his parents basically said the same thing, but he didn't want them to be right, he just wanted this broken heart to heal.

Silvia stood at the door to her son's room, and said a quick prayer before knocking. She heard him say, "Come in," and opened the door. It was tough to see Parker, who was normally so active an energetic, seem so still. "Are you ready?" She asked, hoping he understood that she was asking on several levels.

Sitting up, Parker blew out a breath. "Give me about fifteen minutes and I'll be ready to head over to the house," He answered his mother.

Leaning up against the doorjamb, Silvia's anger began to bubble. "You know you sound like a little boy throwing a tantrum."

"And again," Parker shot back, "we're back to you telling me what an idiot I'm being as far as Jayde is concerned."

On the verge of tears, Silvia pointed to her son, her voice raised, "You know, I never called you an idiot, but I think that you're just letting the happiness you could have had just float away." She looked away for a moment, trying to compose herself, "Life is about how we fight through the crap that's thrown at us, Parker, not about just giving up at the first test."

"Mom," Parker got up. "I know you and Dad are trying to help, but I haven't let her go, she let me go." He turned away to walk into the bathroom and closed the door behind him.

Silvia stood there, and allowed the tears to come.

Jayde was in the middle of serving a couple who were on the island for their honeymoon. Luckily, they arrived after Hurricane Harvey hit. She was telling them about some things to do when she saw Sister Marjorie walk into the shop.

After getting the couple's coffees, she walked over and gave Sister Marjorie a hug.

"That's a lovely hello," Sister Marjorie replied. "Does this mean that you and your young man have made up." The look Jayde wore told her that she'd misjudged the situation. "I'm so sorry, sweetie," She patted Jayde's hand.

Smiling, Jayde replied, "I know you are, and I don't know what happened but I'll deal with it. I'm so excited because my mother's friend, Trisha, is here for a visit."

Sister Marjorie remembered Frannie talking about her best friend during her illness. "Oh, that's lovely," She told Jayde.

As if she knew she was being discussed, Trisha chose that moment to walk into the shop.

Jayde smiled widely, and waited for Trisha to make her way over to them. She gave her aunt a hug, and then began the introductions. "Auntie Trisha, this is Sister Marjorie."

Not standing on ceremony, Trisha leaned down and gave the Sister a hug. "I am so pleased to meet you," She said warmly.

"Please join me," Sister Marjorie told her, "Let's have Jayde get us some yummy chocolate concoctions to drink and we'll chat."

With raised eyebrows, Trisha nodded eagerly. "I'm all for that plan."

Jayde walked away, laughing.

An hour later, Jayde was sitting at the table with Sister Marjorie and Trisha when the Senior Three Amigos came in.

Before long, there were tables pushed together and everyone was chatting.

Jayde likened it to a family reunion except these people only just met. It was a testament to the wonderful people she surrounded herself with. The only people missing were Joe and Parker.

"Where is Joe?" Ginny asked a little while later.

Sighing, Jayde answered, "On one of his super-secret missions."

Trisha was intrigued, "What do you mean?" She asked Jayde.

Gretchen piped up, and answered, "He leaves every day at about the same time and is gone for an hour or two, and no one knows where he goes."

"Interesting," Trisha commented, and took a bite of the muffin she ordered. "Oh my Lord," She gasped, "this is so wonderful."

The group laughed.

Ray told her, "Oh yeah, Joe makes the best baked goods."

Taking another bite, Trisha savored the tastes. "It's so complicated, the tastes."

"He likes to play with spices and flavors," Jayde spoke as she was starting to clear the plates.

Gretchen took a sip of her tea and said, "This is why I need to go to the gym five days a week. Otherwise I'd be sitting in here and eating everything in sight."

Everyone laughed at the comment.

Jayde walked the plates back to the kitchen and set them in the sink. She was turning around to go back out into the shop when she caught sight of her Someday book sitting on the desk. Walking over to it, she frowned. Not remembering that she pulled it out of the drawer, she placed it back inside, intending on asking Joe about it.

When she got back out into the front of the shop there was a good-spirited debate over who was picking up the tab for the group's food and drink. Ray seemed to be trying to be a gentleman, but the women were just not letting him.

She was checking on another customer when the door chimed, and she saw Joe coming back inside. Smiling, she nodded in greeting and took the order from the customers.

Connor came into the shop, and walked around the counter to put his stuff away and put on his apron.

Jayde motioned him over to the table, for introductions. Trisha gave him a wink, and shook his hand. It was funny to see Connor blush.

The group was getting ready to leave so Jayde said, "Hold on, I'd like Aunt Trisha to meet Joe and then you can all go on your way."

She walked into the kitchen, and peeked her head around the corner, "Hey Joe," she smiled. "Can you come out and meet my Aunt Trisha?"

With a grunt, since he was putting away baking supplies, Joe stood up and followed Jayde out to the table.

Jayde made it to the table first, and announced, "So, here's the genius behind your caloric addictions."

The group laughed and were talking. That was, until Aunt Trisha looked up and saw Joe.

"Oh my God," She stood up, almost tripping backward.

Jayde's smile instantly faded. She didn't understand what happened.

Sister Marjorie, Ray, Gretchen, Ginny, and Connor all quieted immediately and didn't say anything.

Joe stood next to Jayde, looking shocked.

Chapter 19

"Frank?" Trisha spoke in barely a whisper. She lifted her hands to her lips, and they were shaking. Tears were filling her eyes.

The group looked from Trisha to Joe.

"Patti?" Joe asked, his voice sounding shaky.

Jayde was pretty sure something pretty epic was going on, but she didn't know what. "Um," She looked at her aunt. "Aunt Trish, are you okay?" She asked.

Nodding, but her eyes still glued on Frank, Trisha felt like her knees were going to buckle. "Oh my Lord," She repeated and sat down.

Within moments, Joe was by her side. "Patti," He said as she knelt down next to her, and asked, "How did you find me?"

Tears were now pouring down Trisha's face. "I wasn't looking for you, Frank, I'm here to see Jayde."

Joe looked over at Jayde, confusion in his eyes.

Jayde knew that, although she really wanted to know what was happening, that they were open for business, and there were customers in the store. But before she could say anything to Connor, Joe stood up.

"Sorry folks," He announced, "We've got to close the shop early, I'm sorry for the inconvenience, and your orders are on the house."

Within minutes, customers had vacated the shop. Connor got up and locked the door behind the last customer and then practically ran back over to the table.

During the few minutes that customers were leaving, no one at the table said anything. No one moved, barely breathed. Looks were exchanged but it was apparent that everyone wanted to know the story.

Connor had just sat down when Joe said to Jayde, "Pull up a chair."

She did as she was asked without comment.

Trisha spoke first, "Frannie and I were best friends in high school. We were vacationing in California when we walked past these guys playing volleyball."

As if on cue, Joe picked up the story. "My Marine Corps unit was on leave before we were supposed to be deployed." He looked at Trisha as if she weren't real, and then said, "And Patti and I met, and my best friend, Will met her friend," he seemed to search for the name, "Marie, right?" He asked Trisha.

Sitting back in her seat, Trisha held her hand over her mouth. The situation was clearing up. "Back then, none of us girls wanted to use our given names." She smiled at Jayde. "I went with Patti, instead of Patricia or Trisha, and your mom went was Marie instead of Francine."

Everyone was so still and quiet that you could hear a pin drop.

A tear slipped down Jayde's cheek. "Will?"

"Back then," Joe explained, "We all abbreviated names. Will was short for Williams."

Her breathing ragged, Jayde looked over at Sister Marjorie. The look the Sister wore was one of shock.

Trisha gently put her hand over Joe's as if she were afraid he wasn't real. "Jayde is Frannie and Will's daughter," She told him.

Joe's head flipped so fast, he had a moment of dizziness. "She's?" He couldn't finish the question.

It couldn't be this simple, Jayde thought to herself. She can't be working for the man who was her father's best friend, could she? "So," Jayde tried to summon the courage, and asked, "You know my father?"

Slowly, Joe nodded.

Everyone gasped, but didn't say anything.

"So," Jayde stood up, and started pacing, "You can contact him and maybe I can meet him."

Joe looked down, and then at Trisha. Finally, he looked back at Jayde, and told her, "When I leave here for my breaks, I go and see him."

Sister Marjorie stood up and went to stand next to Jayde. She suspected what was coming, and wanted to help.

"Really?" Jayde asked excitedly.

Joe looked back down. He had only cried twice in his life; today was the second time. Trisha placed her hand on his back and her touch gave him the courage. "Jayde, I'm sorry, he passed away."

It was if all the air in Jayde's lungs were sucked out. She almost fell, but Ray and Connor guided her into the chair she'd vacated. "Wha, what?" She stammered.

Joe looked around the table, and saw faces of people who cared for Jayde. He loved her too, like a daughter, and now he knew why. "We were deployed and he died while we were there." There was no need for details, it changed nothing.

Trisha began crying. Her heart was breaking for Jayde, but her mind was going one hundred miles an hour. She couldn't believe she'd found Frank after all these years. "Why did you say your name was Frank back then?" She asked.

Joe gave a shy smile, "My given name was Franklin Joseph," he smiled at Trisha. "You did the same thing."

With a nod, Trisha told him, "I did." She looked at Jayde, and then back to Joe, and said, "We didn't know how to reach you."

"I know," He told her, "they deployed us faster than we thought, and we were young and stupid and didn't think about all of that, did we?"

Trisha was crying again, "No, we didn't."

Jayde was torn between watching the scene between Aunt Trisha and Joe and demanding answers about her father.

Sister Marjorie looked around the table. "I'm pretty shell-shocked right now." She announced to the group, and received nods all around. "Why don't we let Joe and Trisha have a few minutes to catch up on details, and then," she looked at Joe and Trisha, "if you two could come up to Jayde's apartment and let her know what she wants to know."

Both Trisha and Joe nodded.

Connor got up and went into the kitchen, followed by Ray, Gretchen, and Ginny, who volunteered to help him clean up.

Sister Marjorie walked Jayde upstairs to her apartment.

Sitting down in the chair, a little while later, Jayde asked again, "Is this really happening?"

"Yes," Sister Marjorie answered as she handed Jayde a cup of tea. "And I think it's beautiful."

Tears filling her eyes again, Jayde nodded, "It is, isn't it?"

An hour later, Joe and Trisha came upstairs. They sat down on either side of Jayde and started filling in the blanks about how everyone met, and then were separated.

"My father told my mother where he was from, so that's why we moved down here." Jayde said quietly.

Sister Marjorie interjected, "And she did find him, she just didn't know it."

They all looked at her.

Joe took Jayde's hand into his, and explained, "I had a lot of guilt over Will's death, since he died trying to save me." He tried to keep his emotions in check. "I go to the cemetery every day to talk to him."

"Your super-secret missions," Jayde told him.

With a smile, he nodded.

Jayde nodded in return, and asked, "Can you take me to see him?"

Joe said, "Yes, but I have to make another confession, Jayde."

Not sure she wanted to know anything else, Jayde told him, "Okay."

"Well, seeing Patti again, and knowing I'd give anything to not have to wait twenty some odd years to see her again, I have to tell you that your young man, Parker, called you the other day. I guess his phone got damaged in the flooding, and he wanted me to tell you that he was okay and to have you call him."

Anger shot up through her, but Jayde contained it. "Joe, why would you do that?" She asked instead.

Looking like a kid in trouble, Joe admitted, "He hurt you and I just wanted to protect you."

Another heavy layer of emotion threatened to envelope Jayde. "Oh Joe," She began crying.

Trisha gave Joe a sharp look, and said, "Jayde, we'll give you some time." She gave her head a nod toward the door, and she and Joe left.

Sister Marjorie sat down, and took a deep breath. "Well, you've had a day now haven't you?"

The way the Sister worded it made Jayde laugh. "I guess you could say that."

"But, you've found your father Jayde." Sister Marjorie said. "It's a Blessing."

Looking down at her cup of tea, Jayde replied, "It's in my Someday book."

Since Sister Marjorie knew about the Someday book, she commented, "And then it came true."

"Falling in love was in there too," Jayde revealed.

Smiling, Sister Marjorie returned, "Well, what are you going to do?"

Parker drove up to the house, and blew out a breath.

They were doing the demo on the house today, and his mom said the foreman requested he be there.

Over the last week, she'd been dictating to him what he needed to do. He grumbled about it, but inside, it was probably the only thing keeping his mind from going crazy.

Getting out of the car, Parker walked up to the house. Evidence of the demolition was everywhere. The garage door was opened and there was already a growing pile of drywall, furniture, and appliances.

As Parker got to the front door, he could hear the buzzing of saws, and people yelling.

Inside, he was told to put on a mask, and one of the workers pointed him in the direction of the master bedroom at the back of the house.

Parker made his way back, still hearing the sound of water squishing under his shoes.

As he entered the master bedroom, he stopped. There was no drywall on the bottom of the walls. The room was completely gutted and didn't even resemble his bedroom. And no one appeared to be in the room either. He made his way through to the closet, to see if anyone was there, but still, nothing.

As he came out of the closet, Parker stopped where he was.

There stood Jayde, hands on her hips, a hard hat on her head, safety glasses on, her mask pulled down to her chin, and a look of censure on her face. "About time you show up, Parker Kinley," She told him sternly. "We've got to decide how to do this house and you should probably have a say in that."

He didn't move, didn't say anything, just stared at her.

Jayde knew she'd have to make the first move.

"Your mom did tell me that you were being rather difficult so I'll make this really easy for you," She took a step toward him. "I prefer to see the sunset from my bed, so we can lay there and see it together," another step. "But, I do realize that maybe that's not what you prefer to do." Another step closer. "And I need a bigger bathroom, this one just isn't quite big enough." Another step. "Are you going to say anything, or am I going to have to design this whole house myself?" She asked, only a foot away from him.

"You can do whatever you want, Jayde," Parker replied. "It's your home too."

Jayde tilted her head as if she was considering his words. "Really?" She asked.

Parker nodded, "Yes, ma'am."

Looking down at her hands, Jayde pulled off her work gloves, "You see, I was told that you called me but someone forgot to pass on the message."

"Bad move," Parker commented.

Nodding, Jayde smiled. "Well, I'd say I'll forgive you for dropping your phone in water if you forgive me for not putting you first."

His composure was now slipping, and Parker wanted to stay strong, "Jayde, you are the most giving person I know."

She shrugged, and replied, "Usually, but not with you."

"And now?" Parker asked her.

She took one more step closer to him so that they were only inches away, but still not touching. "I'm ready, Parker Kinley, to give you everything I have."

Parker looked around, "I'd do the same, but as you can see, not much here."

"You're here," Jayde told him, a tear slipping down her cheek. "And we'll build it all together."

Not wanting to wait a second longer, Parker reached out and pulled her to him. It was like stepping into the sunlight after weeks of darkness. His doubts were lifted off of his heart. "Dammit, woman, I missed you."

Jayde's arms came around him and clamped tightly. Her hat fell off and dropped onto the floor. "I missed you too."

"I love you, Jayde," Parker whispered into her hair.

Jayde smiled. She loved hearing that. "I love you too," She returned, and added, "I found my dad."

Stepping back so he could see her face, Parker was shocked, "What? When? Where is he?"

Smiling at him, and glad that he was willing to forgive her, "We'll talk about that later, right now, just kiss me, will you?"

"Gladly," Parker replied, and brought his lips down to hers.

A week later, Jayde, Parker, Sister Marjorie, Joe, and Trisha were all at the cemetery.

"This is where I go every day," Joe explained to them as they walked up to a grave that had a bench sitting beside it.

Jayde was holding her Someday book, and looked at Sister Marjorie before starting to cry.

"Baby," Parker was getting worried, "What's wrong?"

Sister Marjorie was overcome by emotion as well, and had to take a moment. "Francine came to me, before she went into the hospital, and asked me to come here with her." She looked at Jayde, and gave her a brave smile. "We walked around and she came to this spot. She told me that she wanted to be here, where there was a bench, because she knew that someone would always be nearby."

Still not understanding, Parker looked to Joe.

"I put this bench here when we got back, I wanted to sit and talk with Will." He explained.

Trisha's hand covered her mouth. "Oh my," She gasped. "Their graves are right next to each other."

Joe nodded, trying to get his emotions reigned in. "Looks that way."

Jayde sat down on the bench, and let her tears flow. Parker sat down next to her, and the others walked away to give them some privacy.

She opened her Someday book and found the pages that she wrote, 'find my dad.' "It's so crazy that he was here all along."

Parker was torn up with emotions. "Well, I think now might not be the best time, but I'd like to ask you to marry me, and if this is the closest I'll get to asking your parents' permission to do it, then it will have to do."

Laughing, Jayde looked at him. "I guess I can cross off, 'find true love,' and, 'marry the man of my dreams,' now too.

They sat there, laughing and crying, and finally Parker pulled out a ring. As he slipped it onto Jayde's finger, he knew that as unconventional as their love was, it was perfect for them.

www.ingramcontent.com/pod-product-compliance
Lightning Source LLC
Chambersburg PA
CBHW070832120626
46556CB00002B/730